DASH FOR DUNKIRK

A NOVELLA

DENIS CARON
FRAN CONNOR

ISBN-13: 978-1973712541
ISBN-10: 1973712547
(Paperback Edition)

Characters in this book are fictitious. Any similarity to real persons, living or dead, is coincidental and not intended by the author.

Editing by Rebecca Henderson (www.thekreativspace.wordpress.com)
Cover Design and Formatting by Sarah Orr, *Orr Creative*

Printed and bound in USA
First Printing July 2017
Published by Productivolgy
PO Box 48065 Postal Code N2E4H0

Visit our website
www.DashforDunkirk.com

This book is dedicated to those who paid the ultimate sacrifice in the name of freedom.

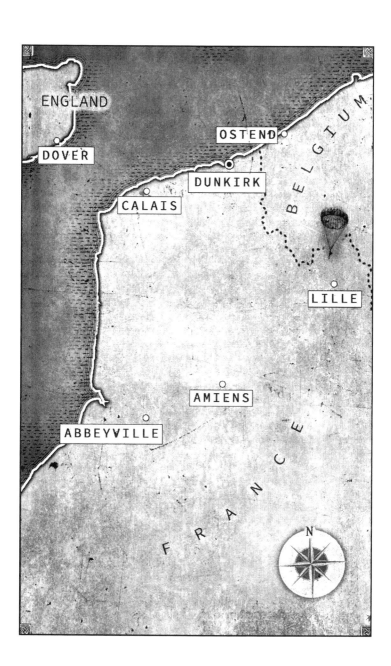

CHAPTER ONE

Northern France: Sunday 26th May 1940

Thwack!

Incredible, I hit it. Not far, but I hit it, so I am not out the first ball. Can't claim it was good play on my part. Didn't even see the ball before it hit the bat. Damned silly game; we didn't play this on the Shankill.

Here comes Larry again with the sun behind him. Sneaky bugger! His blond, curly hair bounces as he roars up to the line. I bet he learned it at Eton. He bowls as if he's shooting down a 109, and he's bagged a few of those in this short war. Who would have thought that I, a working-class lad from Belfast, would be best mates with a rich public schoolboy? It just goes to show that in the close-knit team of an RAF squadron, background matters little. What counts is whether your comrades can rely on you and I hope I have proved my worth. I know Larry has. He shot down a 109 that was on my tail over Amiens.

The ball comes at me so fast I can't even see it.

Missed it this time; there go the wickets with a crash.

'Hard cheese, old chap.' I turn around and see Dickie holding the ball and having a laugh. He's another public schoolboy. Harrow. And I know I can rely on him too. Dickie has that quiet confidence that comes from a privileged background, but he doesn't have an ounce of snobbery. He's good company on a bar crawl around Rouen, though we haven't had the opportunity to go this last week. One Op after another and no sign of stopping Jerry. That's why we play this stupid cricket. Nothing else to do while we wait for our next orders.

It's good that we can still laugh. Things have been very dicey the last few days. We have had our backsides kicked by the Germans. From what I heard, the British and French armies are in retreat over on the Belgian border. I don't know if they will dig in, like in 1914 with trench warfare raging for years. That would be awful. My Da was in that one, and it left its mark on him. Nightmares. I used to hear him scream in the middle of the night. Ma always calmed him down. Poor old Da. He wouldn't harm a spider. In fact, he used to catch them in a glass and let them go outside because he couldn't bear to kill anything. God only knows what he went through in the trenches. God, don't let it come to that again.

Uh-oh. Here comes the station commander. What could it be now?

'Right, that's it. We are off. Complete disaster. I've just had it confirmed that the army is being evacuated. We are to abandon this base and take the ground crew out through Le Havre. You three make your way to Manston. Looks like the Jerries will be taking a trip across the Channel because there is no chance of us stopping them now. Churchill wants all pilots back in Blighty.' He runs his forefinger and thumb through his pencil moustache. That is always a bad sign.

'Yes, sir,' says Dickie upping his role from wicket keeper back to Flight Lieutenant.

'And before you cross the Channel…'

Uh-oh. Here it comes.

'There's a big problem with some our chaps getting out of a jam. Actually, rather a lot of chaps. And rather a lot of jams. The French are holding Jerry back near Lille and again from Abbeyville down to the southeast. It's a long and stretched defence to give our men a chance but they can't hold out much longer and may already have broken. You three are to wallop the Jerries on your way back to Manston. Not sure what good it will do, other than help the morale of our people on the ground. Pick your targets and don't risk the planes. If you can knock out a few of their damned 88s that would be good. They're pulverising our tanks.'

Dickie, Larry, and I look at each other.

He hands a map to Dickie. 'Three Hurricanes are not going to make a huge difference, but we have to try.'

'Yes, sir,' says Dickie throwing a salute.

The station commander strolls off. I hope he and the ground crew make it to Le Havre and find a ship to take them. What a balls up. We've lost a lot of aircraft and more importantly, comrades in this debacle, and now we are all running away. Well, at least it isn't going to be years of trench warfare and for that one should be grateful.

Dickie lowers his six-foot, three-inch athletic frame to sit cross-legged on the grass. He always seems too big to cram into the Hurricane cockpit, but he has two Heinkels and a Junkers for his tally. Dickie is the only one of us who has been to Berlin. He went there in '36 for the Olympics as a high jumper. He saw Hitler. If this all goes wrong for us, we may be seeing Hitler in London. It may be a while before we go to Berlin. The Germans might be visiting London before we visit their capital.

Larry and I sit with him. I pull out my map and Larry finds his.

'Well, here they are. Poor sods. There must be plenty of targets for us.' He points on the map to an area south of the Channel and not far from the Belgian border. 'When I spot a target, we'll attack in single file. Me first, then you, Harry, and then Larry. We can expect a hot reception. I doubt our contribution will help much but...'

'I'm up for it, Dickie,' says Larry.

'Me too.' I am, but I have a feeling that this is all going to end badly.

* * *

In my flying jacket and boots, I climb into my Hurricane cockpit. I have my Webley in my holster, my parachute, and a deep foreboding in my stomach. There is no need for me to cram myself in, even with the parachute. I am only five-foot-eight. It is one of the newly-designed Hurricanes with the steel tube fuselage. They take some punishment. Three days ago, mine had the port side riddled with holes from a Heinkel, but she did not let me down, and I got the Heinkel. Soapy Watson my number one mechanic fixed the damage in half a day. Here he comes now.

'Hi, Soapy. Hope you make it to Manston.'

'Thanks, sir. Smiffy, the adjutant's clerk, just heard Flight Sergeant Carter talking to the Wing Commander. Seems Jerry is heading to cut the army off east of here. Anyway, with any luck I'll see you at Manston. The crate's in good nick and fully loaded with fuel and ammo. Give the bastards hell, sir.'

I put my thumb up and then fire the Rolls Royce Merlin engine. It makes a throaty sound as the exhausts just ahead on each side of the cockpit spit out grey smoke. I throttle back. Soapy pulls the chocks away.

I look across the field. Dickie is fired up and ready and on his other side so is Larry. Here we go then. I feel the oily stomach and slight shake in the hands come on. It's always like this just before we go up. I know Larry and Dickie have the same feeling. We would be fools not to be scared.

In a V-formation, we thunder down the grass runway and up into the blue. Undercarriage up—a quick burst on the four cannons—yes, they are good. Bloody good these Brownings and a match for Jerry's any time. All set. There is not much cloud cover. I reckon we'll be there in half an hour. Any Luftwaffe will spot us easy. With Larry and Dickie, I'm sure we will give a good account of ourselves. Up here, the nerves and the gloom disappear. It's exhilarating.

A voice in my leather flying helmet is the unmistakable upper-class tones of Flight Lieutenant Dickie Davies. He doesn't need to identify himself, but he is a stickler for protocol on operations. That is until it hits the fan. and then he relaxes. 'Apple Baker–Baker–Baker, Apple Monkey–Monkey–Monkey, this is Apple Leader–Apple Leader–Apple Leader, over.'

'Go ahead, Apple Leader, this is Apple Baker, over,' I reply, keeping my eyes on the skies above for any 109s that may be about. We can't have far to go now. It's up to Dickie to choose the target.

'Go ahead, Apple Leader, this is Apple Monkey, over.'

I don't know how Larry was stuck with that moniker.

'Almost there, Apple Baker. I have visual on a target. Looks like an 88 emplacement. I'll go in first, followed by you and then Apple Monkey. Aim for the rear of the 88.'

'Roger that, Apple Leader, Baker over.'

'Roger that, Apple Leader, Monkey over.'

Here we go. I can see the emplacement with its long-barrelled 88 artillery piece. If we can take that bugger out it will give our lads more of a chance.

'Tally-ho.' Dickie goes into a dive with all cannons firing. I see spurts of earth and stones, even from this distance. He's clear and climbing. I don't know if he hit the target.

Now it is my turn. I set my angle, coming in at forty-five degrees, blazing away, and then climb, quickly. Whether I did any damage, I cannot tell, but I bet I put the wind up Fritz.

Larry should be following and then we will circle and come back. This time there will be more of a reception party.

I follow Dickie in an arc and manage to look back. Oh, no! Larry's engine is on fire. Bail out, Larry. You're high enough. No! He's heading north. I hope he makes it. Daft bugger is going to try to save the plane. He's a

Classics scholar like me. 'Come back with your shield or on it,' the Spartan warriors were told, according to Plutarch. Larry's shield is the Hurricane and he's taking it home. Just Dickie and me now.

'Apple Monkey to Apple Leader. Engine on fire and controls sticky. Heading north. Good luck.'

'Apple Leader to Apple Monkey, bail out, Larry. Bail out!'

'Negative, Apple Leader. I'll get the crate home. Good luck.'

'Apple Leader to Apple Baker, Monkey has had it. Follow me. We're going in again.'

'Roger Apple Leader.'

I follow Dickie round. He goes in. Yes! A massive explosion rips through the emplacement. Dickie must have hit some ammunition. I pull out of my dive and climb.

There is smoke coming out of Dickie's engine. Black smoke. Looks serious. 'Apple Baker to Apple Leader, Apple Baker to Apple Leader.'

'Apple Leader to Apple Baker. In a fix, old chap. I'm going to fly north and try to cross over. Got to get the kite back to Blighty.'

Dickie isn't a Classics scholar. He's a biologist of all things, but he's going to get his shield back, too. They may be crazy, but I can't help admiring both Dickie and Larry for their courage. Given a choice, for me, it would be to hell with my kite, much as I love it.

'Apple Leader, you'll never make it.'

'Shadow me, Harry. I'm going to try.'

'Roger, Apple Leader. Good luck, Dickie.'

I will say that for Dickie, he has guts. That engine could blow at any moment. I sit on his tail above him just in case it does blow. It would take me out, too, if I was on his level.

'Baker! Baker! Baker!—Apple Leader—bandits at eleven o'clock.'

I look over to the west. Coming out of the only clouds around and the sun are two 109s. They're coming straight for us. Dickie can't do anything. I will take them both on. I throw one last look over towards Dickie. Flames pour from the engine. For God's sake, bail out, Dickie! I know he can't hear me. There goes the canopy. He's out. Parachute open. There's a chateau down there. I hope we have it. No time to worry about Dickie now. I have a fight on my hands.

I throw the Hurricane into a climb up to twenty-thousand feet. The engine screams. I see the 109s follow. I know they can climb faster than I do. I level off and then dive at the pair. It is my only chance. They will have me for sure if they get behind me. With my four cannons blazing, I hit one of them. It goes into a spiral. I'm happy it is not me in that spiral, but I cannot get used to this killing. The other fires at me from its fuselage cannons. We pass. Me, a cigarette paper, above, him below. That was close.

I saw his face. He is a youngish fellow, late twenties, same as me.

I throw the Hurricane into a loop. I have to stay behind him. Arghh! I feel sick from the motion. Don't throw up. Don't throw up. Eyes on the distant. That's it. Breathe. Breathe. That's better.

He has come round. I dive. Damn! He is behind me. I climb and then veer to port, but he is still with me. I loop. I've tried everything. He's good. I can't shake him off. The thud of his shells hitting the back of my plane sends shock waves down the fuselage. He has me. The steering will not respond. He must have damaged the tail flap. Oh no! The engine is gone. The nose dips. Smoke fills the cockpit. All I hear is the sound of the wind as it whistles by. I will be in a spiral any second.

With a desperate push, I have the canopy off. The air rushes by. I have never bailed out before. Here goes. God help me!

Arghh! It feels like I've hit a brick wall, but it's only air. How hard can air be? My Hurricane drops below me and spirals down. Soapy won't be fixing it this time. No shield for me. My hand trembles but I manage to pull the cord. There's nothing I can do except wait for the tug. Why is time so slow? There it goes. Somebody up there must be watching. All I can hear is a silence so loud it fills my ears. My shoulder hurts like the devil. Maybe I caught it when I bailed out.

There's the 109. It is coming back for the kill. I'm a sitting duck. Well, no, I am not sitting I'm floating. I laugh. No, that's not laughter, it's hysterics.

They say a drowning man's life flashes before him. I'm not drowning, but I see the Shankill in Belfast. There I am, snotty nose and short pants and my Ma donkey stoning the step of our terraced house. She had the cleanest front door step in the street.

I see Theresa Flynn, my first girlfriend. We were not supposed to see each other. She was a Catholic from the Falls. A pretty girl, she had two plaits in her red hair. It makes no sense that our communities were at each other's throats. Looks like it is the end of the road for me now. Joe Kelly said she's married with four children. Funny what you think of when you are so close to meeting your Maker. I thought I would go all religious; instead, I'm blabbering about Theresa Flynn.

Here he comes. I won't shut my eyes. I won't. Will it hurt? Should I draw my Webley? What use would that be? I'd be the first to shoot down a 109 with a pistol. It isn't going to happen. To hell with it! I'll go down fighting. Stories I read as a child about the Vikings dying with their swords in their hands so they could go to Valhalla fills my brain. The Spartans at Thermopylae inspire me to pull the pistol. It won't be Valhalla for me, but—

Here he comes. Red spurts erupt from the cannons. Please let it be quick. Don't injure me badly. Kill me!

With two hands on my gun, I fire at the 109. I know it's stupid. What was the name of that cowboy I saw in a film? John Wayne. That was it. With a Colt .45, he shot a man from the back of a horse at two hundred yards. It only works on film. That's all I saw because I was in the back row necking with Kathy Kelly. Joe said she was married now with three children. All my old girlfriends are married now. I'm going to die without marrying, and I'm not leaving any children behind. That makes me sad. I should have been more responsible instead of seeing how many women I could bed because I had wings on my uniform and they were attracted to the flyboy image. Well, I'm bound for Heaven or Hell so here goes. I empty the chamber at the 109. Useless. It still comes on firing. I hear the shells crack through the air. One wings so close to my ear I feel the wind from it.

The 109 screams past. He missed me. I watch him turn and come back to try again. My pistol is empty, so I shove it back into the holster. 'Keep things tidy' was Ma's motto and in the unlikely event I get to terra firma alive, I may need it.

Funny, I don't feel as scared as I was the first time he came at me. Why? I have no idea. I'm falling through the air under a huge canopy while a man I have never met wants to kill me. This is insane. There go the cannons again. He hasn't hit me yet. Bloody Hell, Wait. He's stopped firing. Must be out of ammunition. Ha-ha! I stick two fingers up at the oncoming plane.

It flashes past. The port wing tip misses me by inches. The turbulence rocks me under and the parachute.I hope it doesn't fold. He's not coming back. Not out of the soup yet, though. If the Jerries are down there, they'll soon start taking pot shots at me. All I can think of is that I don't want to be shot from the ground because the bullet is going to go up my…

* * *

What is that down there? A wood. Fields all around and I am heading for a bloody wood. Can't shift direction; the wind carries me. Probably out of instinct, I pull up my knees. Have to try to save the crown jewels because maybe I will have the opportunity to marry and have children after all.

Shit! I've hit the trees. My 'chute catches in the high branches of an oak and pulls me to a sudden stop that digs the harness into me and hurts like hell. Damn. I am only ten feet from the ground and hanging here like a banana. I scrabble at the harness catch but it will not free.

That bush down there. It moved. Am I seeing things?

No, I am not. Under that foliage is a Jerry helmet and he is pointing a Mauser pistol at me.

'Take it real easy now. Lift your gun from your holster with two fingers and drop it to the ground.'

I don't believe it. The Jerry has a Yank accent. With my thumb and forefinger, I lift out my Webley and drop it to the floor. Anything else would be suicide. It isn't loaded anyway.

'Okay, now try get yourself out of that corset,' he says with a grin.

I tug, pull, eventually release the harness, and drop the ten feet to the ground, where I roll and come up fast. He is ready for me and has the pistol levelled at my chest. This fella knows what he's doing. A less confident person may have just shot me.

I look around. He's on his own. Near where I first saw him are binoculars and a pack radio. He must be a spotter for the Luftwaffe or artillery. Maybe I will get a chance to escape later.

'So, what's a Yank doing in the Wehrmacht? If you don't mind me asking while we stand here, you deciding what to do now.'

'I spent most of my childhood in the States, but I'm German born. You can cut out the questions. I ask them from now on. I'm taking you back to our HQ. I expect they'll want to interrogate you.'

CHAPTER TWO

We head down a deer track through the wood into a glade. The smell of brambles in the air after last night's light rain lifts the space. Such a quiet, pleasant scent seems out of place in the midst of this madness. In the distance, I hear artillery and tanks. You would think they sound the same, but they don't. There's the deep rumble of a monster German M1 siege gun used to blast some poor sods in a concrete defence. Then there's the crack of an 88. I hope one of our tanks is not on the receiving end. At least we got one 88. Not a good trade off though. One 88 for three Hurricanes. At this rate, we will run out of planes before they run out of artillery.

Maybe if the chap behind me gets careless, I'll have the chance to escape. Do I have what it takes to kill a man up close? I've had the training. And I've killed. But that was in the sky at over three hundred miles per hour and at a distance. Doing it by hand, well that's an entirely different kettle of fish. The memories of killing are why Da has the nightmares from the last conflict. Killing and seeing your comrades killed. That's war, and there's nothing noble about it.

'Keep going.' The Jerry prods me in the back with his Mauser.

'How far is it?'

'A few kilometres. Er… about two miles. Why?'

'It's my shoulder. It's giving me jip. I think I bashed it when I bailed out.'

'How about your feet?'

'They're all right.'

'Good! Keep walking.'

'Very amusing. You should be on the stage.'

'Tried that. Only graduated to spear carrier in Aida. Okay, we'll take a rest. Pull up a tree and sit.'

I find a fallen trunk and sit down. My Jerry sits a few feet away still with his Mauser in his hand. He lifts off his coal scuttle helmet. He looks like a regular fellow to me.

'So, who are you?'

'Flying Officer Harry Fitzpatrick RAF. That's all you get.'

'That's okay with me. I'm Feldwebel Gerhardt Asche, Wehrmacht. Can't say I'm pleased to meet you.'

It's really disconcerting talking to a Jerry with an American accent. Just seems so odd. so I can get away 'What made you join the Wehrmacht?'

'What's it to you?'

I shrug. Maybe he doesn't want to be friendly. Why should he? I'm the enemy. 'Drink?' He passes me his water bottle, keeping the gun trained on me.

I take a swig and pass it back. 'Thanks.' Keep smiling. Stay calm. My chance may come.

'I didn't come back to join the Wehrmacht. Last year, I came into Amsterdam on my cargo ship. I was the navigator and First Officer. I thought it would be a great idea to get a train to Hamburg and visit my grandparents. I have a German passport. They conscripted me into the army. You'd think they would have put me in the Navy.'

'Sounds familiar. Find a round hole and stick a square peg in it.'

'Square peg, round hole? Oh, yeah, I get it. So, what's your story? That accent. It's Belfast, ain't it?'

'Yes, I'm from Belfast.'

'Mmmm. They built the Titanic there. You'd think a maritime nation like you British could do better.'

'Hmmm. We also built a lot of other ships.'

'C'mon. I want to get back to my unit before nightfall.'

We set off again through the wood. I check my wristwatch. It's half-past six. It won't be dark until after ten this time of the year. We're bound to be at his unit before then, and I'll have no chance to escape.

We cross a road on the outskirts of a village. The villagers must be staying indoors hoping the war bypasses them. It may if they are lucky. Now we are back in the woods following a deer trail. I'll have to make a move soon.

Ahead, I see a clearing and a barn of some sorts. There's a group of Jerries sprawled around.

We come out of the wood. These Jerries are different from my captor. They're Waffen SS. I can tell by the skull on their black forage caps and black uniforms. Looks as if they are around Company size, around a hundred of the buggers.

They have a fire going. A fat bloke in a dirty white apron hovers over something cooking in a pot. Looks as if they've been in action. Some have bandages on their heads, others have arms in slings, and one man hobbles along with a walking stick. Just the sight of these SS fellas gives me the creeps. It isn't just the forage cap skull badge. I see a half-track with the back flap down. Several bodies, five I think, lie on the floor of the vehicle. I can only see their jackboots. A tarpaulin covers the rest of them. They may want to take their revenge on anyone they can get their hands on, and it looks like that could be me.

Over at the side of the barn, stretched out on the ground face down, I see two bodies in British uniform. They've been shot in the back of the head. Bastards!

A chap, I think maybe an officer, saunters over slapping a stick against his jackboot. My Jerry gives him an army salute.

'Heil Hitler!' says the officer with his free hand extended in the Nazi salute.

He's around six feet tall with broad shoulders and a few days' growth of stubble on his sour face.

My Jerry says something to him that I can't understand. The officer yells back at him, points at me and then at the barn. I don't know what the hell is going on but now my Jerry shakes his head. The officer grabs him by the lapels and shoves the stick in his face. Shit! He's pushed the officer in the chest. Christ, that could be a capital offence.

The officer throws away the stick and draws a Walther P38 pistol from a holster at his side. Oh God help me.

The other SS soldiers stop what they are doing. There's a buzz running through the ranks. I could end up like those two British fellas. An oily feeling spreads through my stomach. I know what it is, fear. Take it easy, Yank. Don't antagonise the bastard any more.

The SS officer strides over to me. What's he going to do? What should I do? There's nowhere to hide. Well, if this is the end of the road for me, I'm going out with dignity. I stand my ground and stare at the officer. He raises his pistol to my head. Oh Shit!

My Jerry shouts something. Who's he shouting at? Not at the SS officer.

Out of the corner of my wide open eye, I see a soldier in a long grey leather coat striding over towards us. From the markings on his shoulders I think he must be a colonel or higher. He doesn't look too friendly either. Ah, he's not SS or Wehrmacht. He's a Luftwaffe Oberst. I recognise the insignia, two lines with what looks like three rows of two canine teeth above on a wine-coloured square. Yes. Luftwaffe. What's he going to do?

The Oberst barks orders at the SS officer. The SS officer shouts back, red in the face.

My Jerry grabs me by the collar, whacks me on the back of my head with his fist and shoves me forward. He hits me again and pushes me into the wood. Neither blows hurt much. He must have pulled his punches.

Once in the wood, he says. 'Sorry about that. Had to make it look real.'

'What was all that about?'

'Keep walking. And quickly. Lucky for you the Luftwaffe were there.'

'Bloody lucky. What's a Luftwaffe officer doing wandering around amidst the SS?'

'They've captured a French aerodrome near here.'

We pick up the deer track again and continue through the woods. The sound of German artillery is nearer now, and I am even further behind enemy lines. That M1 piece can't be more than a mile away. I don't know where its target is, but I can feel the ground shake from wherever the shells are coming down.

What's that? I can hear grenades and shooting. Sounds like a Schmeisser. And a couple of rifles. What is going on? It's coming from the clearing we left only about five minutes ago. 'What's happening?'

'Stop. Sit down for a minute.'

I sit on the ground and lean against an old oak. The shooting and explosions carry on. My Jerry has a woeful expression on his face. I have a horrible feeling I know what's just happened.

'The Waffen SS, they're shooting the POWs. The officer wanted me to put you in the barn with the others. I told him to fuck off. It's wrong. Very wrong. Stupid bastards. The Luftwaffe agreed with me.'

'They're shooting prisoners? Oh my God! That's contrary to the Geneva Convention. I saw two with bullet holes in the back of their heads.'

'I don't think those assholes understand the Geneva Convention.'

'Why didn't you leave me there with them?'

'I would have no hesitation in shooting you in self defence if you tried anything but killing guys in cold blood, no, that ain't right. I don't want any part of this world domination bullshit. And I don't have anything against Jews either. I grew up with some Jewish friends. I just want to go home to New York. But I can't. If I desert, they will catch me and shoot me.'

'Why not surrender and come back to our lines with me? You will be a POW, and they will treat you according to the Geneva Convention.'

'No chance. Maybe they would treat me okay, but your lot are finished. I'm not sure what would happen to me after your side surrenders. I could be shot by our guys for surrendering. No, this is a mess, but I'll stay on my side for now. Perhaps I'll get a chance to get away some other time. Depends on where they send me after we've beaten you British and the French.'

'So what are you going to do? Will they shoot me when we get to your unit?'

'No, we're Wehrmacht, not SS. I need a pee. Stay there while I go for one.'

He tramps through the wood and disappears behind a tree. What did he mean when he said he would not hesitate to shoot me if I tried anything?

I have to risk it. I can't go back the way we came, or I'll run into the SS. I have a rough idea where I am. The low sun over there tells me that is west, so I need to head north to the Channel. I don't know how far it is or what's between here and there. What I saw of the land from up there, there's a lot of open fields between the woods. It's risky but, what the hell, go for it!

Slowly, I climb to my feet. There's no track north. I ease my way through brambles and fallen branches.

If I try to run, I'll probably fall over something. I turn to see if the Jerry is going to shoot. I can't see him. The ground is a little clearer here. I pick up speed. Another glance over my shoulder. Still no sign of him. After a hundred yards I realise the Jerry really has let me go. I hope he makes it back to America. Those SS bastards didn't need to kill the prisoners. It wasn't as if it were in the heat of battle. Cold-blooded murder.

This war is getting dirtier. That 109 pilot tried to shoot me down after I bailed out. We've had an unwritten rule; we shoot down their plane or they shoot down ours. We don't try to kill the pilot after he's bailed out. And those idiots in the SS kill prisoners. I won't let this destroy my principles though. I'm not going to kill unless there is no other choice.

* * *

I trudge on through the night. If I keep moving in the dark, I can hide in the day. How far do I have to go? I keep crossing open fields between clumps of forest. At least the clouds dim the moonlight. Exhaustion creeps in. I can't see much in this patch of trees and trip over fallen branches. My throat feels like an Egyptian mummy's armpit, and I could do with something to eat. I haven't eaten since breakfast. What happened to Dickie and Larry? I hope they made it. I know Dickie bailed out successfully, but whether Larry made it back to England… I don't know.

Through the undergrowth, I stumble and spot something ahead. Shit! I've wandered into the German army. There's a whole bloody camp of them. The pale moonlight shines on four 88s. I can see three, no four half-tracks. There's an open topped staff car next to them, a Mercedes. Hellfire, I'm in it now.

I hit the ground and crawl as close to a fallen tree trunk as I can manage. The earth smells damp, rotting leaves, the odour of death. They're quiet in the camp, but they must have sentries. Perhaps the one in this sector fell asleep. Come the morning they'll find me here, and if I try to retrace my steps, I could run into a patrol or a wide-awake sentry. Bloody hell!

As I lie here bemoaning my luck, a sudden thought comes to my mind. Yes, it's a crazy one. Well, more idiotic perhaps. Those half-tracks must hold the ammunition for the 88s. They won't have stacked the ammo behind sandbags because this looks like a blitzkrieg unit for fast forward movement. And boy were the bastards fast. Outpaced our lads so easily. I think that's a pile in the fourth half-track.

To go north, I must get through these lines. On my belly, I slide like a snake keeping as close to the ground as I can and my eyes and ears alert to any threat that I may come across. I hope they can't hear my beating heart. I have to do this, to survive; that's what I tell myself.

A sentry leans against the first half-track with a fag in his hand. His rifle, complete with a bayonet, stands propped against the side of the vehicle. I used to have a rabbit's foot for luck when I was at University; I wish I had it now. Jill Reagan gave it to me when I left Belfast. She's married now with two children. For Christ's sake, Harry shut up and concentrate.

I crawl to the fourth half-track and wriggle underneath. He hasn't seen or heard me. Damn. I don't know where the fuel filler is on these machines. To avoid blowing the whole thing up, it must have some protection. What now? I look at the Mercedes and, yes! There's the filler cap on this side. But will it be enough and is it close enough to the ammunition? There's only one way to find out. If not, at least it should create a diversion. I crawl forward and then slide out where the tracks end.

If the sentry comes along, he's bound to spot me.

I rummage in my pocket and pull out a handkerchief. Ma always insisted I had a clean one. Clean handkerchief and clean underpants in case I got run over. She didn't want a red face at the hospital she would say. I made sure I had a clean hanky before I went up on this hopeless mission with Dickie and Larry. If I get this wrong, my underpants won't be clean. From my other pocket,

I withdraw a packet of Swan Vestas. They're part of my survival kit for lighting fires. Well, this is going to be one hell of a fire!

The sentry is coming. I can't get back under the half-track. With all my strength, I drag myself beneath the Mercedes. Thank God it has good ground clearance. Good old Jerry engineering.

He's turned and now heading back. Now is my chance. I roll out from under the staff car and, on my knees, unscrew the petrol filler cap. There's every likelihood that I will blow myself to Kingdom Come but I can think of no other way.

With shaking hands, I stuff one end of the handkerchief into the filler. Thanks, Ma, for making it a big one. The smell of petrol hangs in the air.

I light the makeshift fuse with a match. The strike and the glow must alert the sentry. My dash to cover could win me an Olympic medal.

Just as I throw myself to the ground behind a tree, a crump and then a flash fills the air. Yes! The staff car burns. I hear shouts. Panic. Yes! Got you, you bastards!

From behind my tree, I peer around. People are running, caught in the flickering light from the fire like in an old film reel. The Mercedes is well ablaze, and it's spread to the half-track. That's burning too. Great! Better get the hell out of here before that lot goes up and takes me and the German army with it.

I roll over to stand up. A bayonet stabs the tree where I was moments before. There's a Jerry glaring down at me. He pulls the blade from the tree and strikes again, but I'm ready for him. A kick in the back of the knee sends him buckling to the ground, and as he goes down, I grab the rifle barrel and stock. With a massive effort, I twist the weapon from his grasp as he lies spread out on his back, helpless.

Now I have the rifle and bayonet pointed at him. We did bayonet practice in initial training though we were pilots, not soldiers. What did the sergeant say? Stick him in the belly, not in the chest. The bayonet may get stuck in the rib cage. The belly, every time. Thrust, twist, pull.

I raise to strike. The man closes his eyes. What would my Da do? What did he do in the trenches in this position? Would he have killed the man? I spin the rifle and bring the stock down on the Jerry's nose. I hear it break. Blood gushes. Should I have stabbed him? He won't be winning any beauty contests for a while with that smashed nose, but he'll live.

Boom! Boom! Boom!

The earth shakes. Shrapnel skims through the trees. Debris falls from the sky. How's that for a lucky sod? This is my chance.

I skirt around the pandemonium and clear the front line of the German emplacement. Now I'm running for my life northwards, towards Britain.

Unfortunately, there's a stretch of water between here and there and maybe several German Divisions.

* * *

Two hours have passed since I blew up the ammunition in the German camp. I'm just about done in. What time is it? Two-thirty. Probably another couple of hours to sunrise. Keep going.

What's that over there in the clearing? A cottage. If it isn't in enemy hands, perhaps I could get something to eat and drink.

Take it easy. You don't know who is in there. Could be Jerries or some nervous farmer with a shotgun. I creep into the yard. All is quiet. There's a small barn and a water pump outside. That'll do for a start. I pull the pump handle up and down. Damn, it squeaks. Water gushes out to splash on the cobblestones underneath. In the silence of the night it sounds like Niagara Falls. Not that I've been there.

Suddenly I hear the gaggle of ducks or geese from within the barn. It's geese. I recognise that noise; it's like laughter. They had some on a farm where I used to pick strawberries during the school holidays.

Damn!

A window opens in the cottage. The frightened voice of a woman pierces the night. I must calm her. If there are Jerry patrols nearby, they'll hear and come to investigate.

Across the yard I race. 'English, Madame, English.' Shit! She's holding a shotgun. I put up my hands. 'English, English.'

She says something in a high-pitched tirade, but I have no idea what.

I think I may have got through to her because she's backed away from the window. Now I can't see her. Better stay here and keep still until I know what she is doing. Alarming her may get me blasted with the shotgun. That would be a humiliating way to go after what I've been through.

A light comes on in a downstairs room.

Metal scrapes on metal. The door opens a little. The woman still has the shotgun. She beckons me to come in. I think she's realised I am no threat. I'm bloody sure she's a threat to me but she has the gun so I'd better take it easy.

The downstairs is one large room with a black range at one end; a scrubbed pine table holds an oil lamp from where the light comes. There're two chairs by the table and two old armchairs by the range. Halfway along the back wall stands a rickety staircase. The floor is dirt, I think. Whatever she cooked last night must have had a lot of garlic in it judging by the odour in here.

The woman isn't old. I would put her in her early forties, but the weather and toil have left their marks on her proud and remarkably gentle face.

Over what I can see is a thin body she wears a heavy dressing gown and has a white cotton cap on her long brown hair. There are wisps of grey in those tresses. She points to an armchair by the range. I sit as instructed. Still, she talks away in French, and I understand not a word. She has a mellifluous voice.

The woman leans the shotgun against the table and opens a cupboard, from which she pulls a piece of cheese and half a baguette. Then she lifts out a bottle of wine and wooden cup that she fills from the bottle and then hands the wine, bread and cheese to me. She's smiling.

'Merci.' That's about the limit of my French.

The elements have cracked her hands and toughened them like leather.

The woman sits in the chair opposite and watches me eat. Whatever must she be thinking? If only I could talk to her; she may know where the Germans are so I could avoid them.

On a shelf above the range, I see two photographs of soldiers in French uniform. One has a black ribbon around the frame. It's faded with age. The man has a huge Gallic moustache and looks to be in his twenties. I would say he was a soldier in the last war and judging by the ribbon, a dead one. Probably her husband. Perhaps she has been a widow since the last war. It must be lonely for her. The other soldier I think may be her son and he's in a more modern uniform. I point to the second photo. 'Er, your son?'

'Mon fils.'

I think that means he's her son.

She points to the first photo. 'Mon mari.' Yes, that probably means he's her husband. One has to presume her son is away with the French army. This poor woman is running the farm on her own. Well, once the Germans get here they will relieve her of all her livestock, that's for sure.

The wine is a little rough but it washes down the slightly stale baguette and soft cheese.

The woman smiles and her face lights up with happiness. I really think she is glad to have company even it may get her shot by the Germans.

She points to the stairs. I doubt she has romance on her mind, at least not with a passing stranger who can't even talk to her in her own language.

The stairs creak as I climb. They lead into another large room. Only one. She comes up behind me with the oil lamp.

She has invited me, a stranger, into her house and now her bedroom.

An iron bedstead with brass knobs on the four corners lies with the head against the wall. A small space on both sides under the sloping roof would barely give one room to get in and out.

'I go.'

She shakes her head. There's that smile again; she unbuttons her top.

We go back to bed.

* * *

We get up after a while, hungry for something to eat. I load the range with logs and light it. Soon she has two omelets ready. We sit down at the table and eat. I don't think I have ever tasted an omelet so good. The wine tastes excellent too.

I don't feel bad about what happened last night and again this morning. I didn't take advantage of her. Passing strangers who are able to bring a little comfort to each other in this dreadful world. But I have to go.

'Mariette, I have to go. I have to find the British and get to England.'

'Enger-engerland. Oui! Engerland.' She nods. Did she understand? 'Engerland, oui.' Again, she nods and then climbs the stairs.

Has she got the wrong message?

I hear her moving around up there and then she comes back down carrying my flying jacket and boots.

'Engerland, oui! Bon chance.'

How do I repay her kindness? I have nothing to give her. A handshake seems so feeble after what we have shared. I step forward and kiss her on both cheeks. 'Merci, Mariette.'

'Bon chance.' She smiles. I think maybe she will know how to handle the Germans.

* * *

I don't want to travel in daylight, but I couldn't stay in Mariette's cottage any longer. And I may be a fit young man but Mariette's appetite, well… From here I must tread carefully and keep to the woods where impossible though it seems, there are more open fields here than there were back there. At least the hedgerows on the country lanes are high.

I trudge along what appears to be a farm track. The hedges give me some cover, but it also stops me from seeing if anyone approaches from the fields. I should hear a tank, but I wouldn't hear a patrol. Must keep alert. How much further before I get to our lines? Are we still holding back the Germans? I know the army was heading for the coast with a view to evacuation. Have they abandoned France already? Keep going.

A steady rumble fills the air behind me. I dive into a ditch at the side of the track and look up. I see four Dornier Do 17s, flying low. They're unmistakable, with their twin tail fins, two engines, and a glass bubble on the front where a machine gunner sits. They carry six machine guns and are hellishly difficult to attack, like a hedgehog. The 'flying pencil' they call them. Long and sleek. From what I know about them they carry four

500-pound bombs. They will make a mess of wherever they go. I think they are headed north. That means our lads are going to get a pasting. Let's hope the RAF is waiting for them, though I suspect Churchill is keeping them in reserve for the fight to come. Being down here, I feel so useless. I must get back to England, so I can do my bit. I check my watch. Six-fifteen. It will be dark in about three hours, then I shall be safer unless I stumble into another Jerry camp.

The sight of the Dorniers spurs me on. I break into a run.

In the distance, I hear the deep thud of bombs coming from the direction in which the German planes flew. I can't tell how far away they are. I check my watch. Six-twenty. That's five minutes since the Dorniers went over. They cruise around 200 mph. As a very rough estimate, that means they are bombing around fifteen to twenty miles away. So, we still have some army left if they are bombing. Maybe they are attacking behind our lines, and we have units further forward. I'd better get a shift on. There's a good chance I am going to make it.

With gritted teeth, I set into a pattern. Five minutes running and then five minutes fast walking. Keep it up. That's why we did all that physical training. Thankfully, I'm back in woodland.

For three hours, I keep up the pace, and I don't see another living soul. Where is everybody? The locals must be keeping their heads down. The British and French are running away, and the Germans… I don't know. What the hell are the Germans doing? I thought they would be all over this country by now with nothing to stop them.

I'm at the edge of the wood. The sun has disappeared into its underworld leaving the last rays of light that will soon be gone. There's a cut hay field. I expect the farmer is more interested in staying alive than bringing in the hay. Anyone watching will see me cross it. I still haven't seen any sign of the Germans though I can hear them blasting away with artillery a few miles east of here. If there is a sniper in the woods, he will get me for sure. I should be near our lines by now though I know they are too often what we call 'fluid'.

What's that building over there? It's the chateau near where Dickie bailed out. Is it in British, French, or German hands? I'll wait for proper darkness before I find out.

My shoulder still hurts though it didn't cause a problem last night or this morning so it can't be serious.

I find a dry piece of ground under an oak tree and sit down to wait for nightfall.

It's cold and my body shivers for warmth. I must have fallen asleep. What time is it? Twenty past eleven and it's dark. Now is my chance. As I get to my feet, my knees click, and the muscles in my legs groan. It has been a long day. A smile creeps across my face as I think of Mariette. I could do with a drink and something to eat.

Plenty of cloud cover obscures the moonlight. Here goes. I set off across the field. The smell of cut damp hay pervades the night air. As I make my way up the slight incline on the far side to the chateau, I see movement. This is the moment of truth. If it is Jerry, I'm in trouble.

'Halt! Who goes there?'

A surge of real joy shoots through my body. That's a British voice!

'Friend. Flying Officer Fitzpatrick RAF.'

'Step forward, friend, with your hands in the air.'

I move towards the voice, but I can see only a faint outline in the darkness.

'Stop there.'

I stand with my hands in the air. I've come this far. To be shot by my own side would be foolish, to put it mildly.

'Who won the 1939 FA Cup Final?' demanded the voice.

'Portsmouth.'

'All right, sir. Come forward.'

I move toward the shadowy figure.

The soldier chuckled. Only as I stand next to him

do I notice that he has one arm in a sling and a pistol in the other hand.

'You've made it just in time, sir. We're pulling out in the morning. Well, the walking wounded are. This is a temporary hospital. We're leaving the badly injured for the Jerries to look after. We can't move 'em.'

'I see. How do I get in?'

'Just over there, sir. There's another guard at the door so step carefully.'

I make my way in the direction he sent me. I can't see the other guard, but I can see his glowing cigarette end. He'd get a roasting off his sergeant if he saw that glow but I'm more interested in getting inside and having a drink and something to eat than balling out a squaddie.

'Flying Officer Fitzpatrick approaching.'

I walk forward with my hands up.

The soldier salutes and then wobbles. He has a crutch under his left arm and his left leg in plaster. His Lee Enfield .303 stands against the wall.

I saw this Empire style chateau from the air yesterday—or was it the day before? I'm having trouble remembering its black slate roof, turret at one end, and grey stone walls stand out against the countryside. The gardens appear well kept though I wasn't taking that much notice due to the circumstances up in the blue. It looks quite grand. I wonder who lives here.

I push open the door. There's a curtain behind to keep the blackout, so I close the door before I move the curtain.

Inside, it's bright from electric lighting.

As I look around, I see the entrance hall has a chandelier hanging from a country scene painted on the ceiling. An elegant wooden staircase rises from the black and white tiled floor. On the walls of the hall are portraits, presumably ancestors, in various poses including a Napoleonic officer on a white horse. I can imagine the equestrian entertaining the local gentry and those aristocrats who kept their heads after the Revolution. On the wall to the left hangs a collection of antique firearms. We've since discovered more efficient ways of killing each other.

Over near the staircase, behind a desk, sits a woman dressed in a Red Cross nurse's uniform. She's staring at me. I have to say she is quite a looker with her light brown hair tucked up under the unflattering hat.

'Where have you come from?'

What a lovely accent. She's French, not British. Unlike Mariette, she speaks English.

'A good question. Somewhere south of here.'

'How can I 'elp you?' She has deep brown eyes.

'I could do with something to eat and drink. Could someone look at my shoulder? I hurt it when I bailed out.' Her hands are ring-less and do not look as if she has used them for manual labour like Mariette.

'Come.' She stands up. The nurse seems tall for a French woman; I'd say about five ten. The uniform does no justice to what I can tell is a good figure. She has that air of class you see on the front pages of fashion magazines on the dentist's waiting room table.

I follow her through a door and along a wood-panelled passage. The walls have more portraits and some landscapes. My boots make an echo on the stone-flagged floor.

She takes me into a big kitchen with a black range at one end and a sink at the other. In the middle stands a long pine table with eight wooden chairs on the grey flagstones. Lines of gleaming copper pans hang from the ceiling. In one corner, dangling from a hook, I see a dried leg of ham.

'We' ave a little food left. That's all I can give you tonight. Sit down.'

I sit at the table.

The nurse lifts down the leg and carves off several slices before replacing it on the hook.

She brings me a plate with the 'jambon,' some dried sausage, a baguette and a bottle of beer. The drink slides down my dry throat.

'The soldiers are leaving tomorrow if the transport arrives. I'm sure Major Driscoll will let you go with them.'

'Major Driscoll?'

'Mmmm, he is the doctor here.'

'The soldier outside said they are leaving the seriously wounded.'

'Yes. Major Driscoll 'as made the selection. It is so sad that some of the men must stay here and be taken prisoner. But they are too badly hurt to be moved. I 'ope the Germans will take care of them.'

'Earlier today, near here, one of my squadron bailed out. Did he come here?'

'An RAF pilot? We did take a pilot in. I do not know if it is the man you look for. He had two broken legs and internal injuries from a bad landing. Flight Lieutenant Davies is his name. We watched him come down. Up in the sky, there was a, what do you call it? A dogfight.'

'How bad is he?'

'I'm afraid he is too bad to go with the evacuation.'

'Can I see him?'

'Of course. But not until the morning. He is upstairs in the ward, and everyone is sleeping. I don't want them disturbed. I think you need to eat your food and let me 'ave a look at your shoulder.'

It doesn't sound too good for poor old Dickie. He has a wife and two children back home in Surrey. I suppose I can take a message back to them. Leaving him here doesn't sound like the right thing to do, but if I stay, I'll be in the bag too. Surely the Jerries wouldn't shoot an injured man. But…

I finish off my supper though my appetite has faded with the news of Dickie.

'So, come with me, and I look at your shoulder. Major Driscoll is busy. I will only call him if I cannot deal with your injury.'

I follow the nurse through the chateau's many rooms. Most of them have dustsheets covering the furniture. I haven't seen any of the patients or other nurses. I suppose they are all asleep upstairs or wherever the wards are in this vast place.

We come to a library with stacks of books on all four walls. I see an enormous stuffed fish in a display case. I think it's a carp. I miss fishing in the loughs back home. I've never caught anything as large as the carp. There's a big window with a blackout curtain. I wonder what the view is from here in daylight.

In the centre of the room stands a makeshift examination table.

'Take off your shirt and jacket and lie on the table, face down.'

I strip to the waist and lie down on my front. She runs her hands over my shoulder; they feel soft and warm as she massages my back. Much softer than Mariette's, but I don't want to be making comparisons.

'Does it hurt?'

'No.'

'Does that hurt?' She squeezes my shoulder blade hard.

Pain shoots down my back. I stifle an unmanly yelp. 'Yes, that hurts.'

The nurse pulls my left arm horizontal and then raises it. 'Does that hurt?'

'A little.'

She does some more stretching and massaging. I am enjoying the sensation. A little smile of amusement crosses my lips. Here am I, a pilot on the run from crazy SS and the German army and in the last twenty-four hours two women have massaged me and more. Now that is what I call a result!

'There is nothing broken. You 'ave bruising but that is all. You can get dressed again.'

I slip off the table and put my shirt back on. I leave my jacket on the table.

'Come with me. I find you a place to sleep.'

The nurse takes me up the stairs and along a corridor to a door at the far end. I push open the door. It's a tastefully decorated bedroom with a four-poster bed that has a tapestry back. I wonder who has slept in this bed down the years. Napoleon perhaps? Red flock wallpaper adds to the ambiance. A table lamp with a maroon shade gives the only light, but it is enough to see the antique furniture and more paintings. The floorboards are dark stained. Though not an expert I would say they were cherry wood and have the patina of age. I wish my Ma could see me now! 'Playboy of the Western World,' she used to call me and laugh when I came home from University. I don't think she knew the story of that play by Synge.

My bedroom back home in Belfast is nearer to Mariette's style than this one.

'May I ask your name?'

'Mademoiselle Chappelle.'

'Are you going to tell me your first name?'

'Why do you want to know my first name?'

'I'm just trying to be friendly. My name is Harry.'

She relaxes and smiles. 'My name is Solange.' It's such a sweet smile.

'This is some place the medics have commandeered. Who owns it?'

'It was not commandeered, as you say. The owner offered it to the British and our own soldiers as a temporary hospital. He did not realise how temporary it was to be.'

'Sounds like an all right chap. What's his name?'

'You English, so many questions.'

'I'm not English. I'm Irish.'

'Oh! Well, I do not think that makes any difference. If you really need to know who owns the chateau; it is Henri Chappelle.'

'Chapelle? Any relation?'

'Yes, he is my father. Goodnight.' She walks out and shuts the door, quietly.

Solange seems like a nice woman, but I doubt I shall get to know her if I am to leave in the morning. Anyway, she is way out of my class. I'm a Belfast working class lad who has made good but not that good

I throw my clothes on an antique chair and climb into the bed. I think it must have a feather mattress it is so soft.

* * *

Tuesday 28th May 1940

A sound outside the door wakes me. It's dark. The blackout curtains are still drawn. Someone is knocking. 'Come in.'

The door opens, letting in some light from the corridor. A soldier enters, carrying a mug. I hope it's tea and not that strong French coffee. Around his head, he wears a bandage.

'Mornin', sir. The Doc wants to meet you. Solange told him you arrived in the night. Cuppa tea here and there's toast downstairs. That's about all there is for breakfast.'

'Thanks.'

The soldier hobbles over to the curtains and draws them back. It's a sunny day. He limps out of the room without another word.

I find a bathroom down the corridor and do my best to wash up in the sink. There's a bath but when

I turn the tap the pipes rattle, and nothing comes out.

Downstairs, I find the kitchen where Solange gave me supper. She's there, looking fresh and clean. I suppose her bath works. Instead of the nurse's outfit, she's wearing a pair of black slacks, and a short-sleeved white top. She is very elegant. The bloke in the major's uniform with her must be the Doc.

'Good morning, Flying Officer Fitzpatrick, I believe?' The Doc offers his hand, and I shake it. He's tall, about six feet with a grey moustache and receding hair the same colour. He's more avuncular than Major.

'Good morning, sir.'

'Solange tells me you have a shoulder injury, but it's only bruising. That's fortunate because we are short of able-bodied staff here. I'd like you to help me get the walking wounded out of here when the transport arrives.'

'Of course.'

'Solange also tells me that Flight Lieutenant Davies is from your squadron.'

'That's right, sir. I'd like to see him if that is possible.'

'Yes, Solange will take you to him shortly. We have another patient whom you may know. He's in the same squadron as the Flight Lieutenant, Pilot Officer Latimore.'

'Larry? Here? How is he?'

'I'm afraid he is doing very poorly. He has severe burns and damaged lungs. Some of our retreating soldiers found him and brought him in.'

'He should have bailed out sooner. Brave, silly bugger! Er… sorry, Miss. I'd like to see him too if that's possible.'

'Of course. I don't know if you have any more information but how far away are the Germans?'

'Not far. I don't think there are any of our people between them and us; at least, I didn't see any. As best as I can understand, there are three Jerry columns. One to the east, west, and south. They're trying to cut off the British retreat, and they may well succeed. The French army holds the line to the west of here across northern France down to the Swiss border. Well, they did. I don't know if they still do. I don't know about the Maginot line. Jerry disregarded Belgium's neutrality and came through there. They'll just outflank Maginot if they haven't already. Somebody made a right balls up, er… sorry, Mademoiselle, when they built that white elephant.'

'So the Germans will be here soon. I just hope the transport arrives in time. We are to make our way up to Calais.'

'How long ago were you told to do that?'

'A few days ago. Have things changed?'

'I'm not sure but I think Calais will have fallen.'

'Dear God.'

'We need to get some up to date information. Do you have contact with any of our so-called commanders?'

'Yesterday there were several battalions a few miles north of here trying to sort out some kind of defence but I don't know if their commanders will have any better information. We'll need to know before we set off. The phones are not working. I'll have to send someone to find what's happening.' The Doc strides out of the kitchen, leaving me alone with Solange.

She cuts a slice of bread. 'Would you like it toasted?'

'No, thanks. Just like that will do.' The Germans are about to invade the chateau, and we're discussing bread.

I eat it while she sips a mug of coffee.

'If it isn't taking you away from your duties, I'd like to see my friends now.'

'Certainly. Follow me.'

We make our way through the chateau. I can see out from the windows now that the blackout curtains are drawn. The garden is lovely, and though the land around here is rather flat, in the distance, I can see a slight rise. The fields are yellow and green. Will they harvest whatever grows out there? Such a waste. If I remember correctly, this area is known as the 'Fatal Highway,' where down the centuries invaders have marched into France across these flat lands. I'm a pilot, not a soldier, but even I can see how the Panzers have managed to cut through this terrain so rapidly. Our Matilda tanks have earned a good reputation against the Panzers but the 88s are destroying them. At least I've put some out of action.

We climb the magnificent staircase. Several doors lead off the corridor. Solange takes me into what I can see was once an impressive bedroom. Now, there's a row of four improvised beds each holding a man. There's Dickie next to a chap with his face in bandages. That must be Larry. Oh, poor sod. I can't see any of his blond hair.

'Dickie!'

'Bugger me, Harry, what are you doing here?'

'They got me, too. But I got one of them.'

'Well done. That's Larry next door. He's still asleep. Poor sod is badly burned and his lungs too.'

'I heard. Poor Larry. How are you, Dickie? Are you in much pain?'

'Well, you know what they say, only when I laugh.'

That's Dickie. He takes it all and never complains. He was always the one in charge in our little team of three. Both up in the air and down on the ground. Now he's lying there battered and broken. He's still twice the man I'll ever be.

Solange pours a glass of water and hands it to Dickie. 'C'mon, you need to drink plenty of water.'

'Who can argue with Solange?' He grins and then winces in pain.

There's an old wooden chair in the corner; I pick it up and carry it over to the side of Dickie's bed. Solange checks the other patients.

'So, Dickie, has the Doc said anything to you about evacuation?'

'Yes. I'm not going. He said it was too risky. Apparently, I have some damage inside as well as my legs.'

'What happened?'

'I came down all right until the last eight feet. A gust of wind caught my chute and dragged me into a wall. There was nothing I could do. Lucky it was in the chateau's grounds. They took me in quickly. The Doc worked wonders. Shame about Larry. He's staying too.'

'We're just waiting for the transport to take the walking wounded.'

'Harry, if I give you a letter, could you get it to Mary for me when you're back in Blighty?'

'Of course I will.'

I spend the rest of the morning helping the Doctor get together what he needs for the move. Boxes, bottles, and bandages I stack in the entrance hall by the main door. Some of the able but wounded soldiers help. They're a sorry lot with limbs in plaster or slings. Many head injuries. Though mostly British, there are a few French and one Belgian with a bandage over his eye. There's no panic. As best they can in light of their injuries, they help the Doc. One of the British squaddies, a short chap, sits on the stairs playing a mouth organ; badly, due to only one working hand.

The hospital staff is few. I've seen four French nurses and some local women helping them. They seem a dedicated bunch. I don't know what will happen to them when the Germans come. They'll probably be forced to work in the military hospitals.

The Doc strides into the hall. 'Well done, Harry. We have sixteen to evacuate plus you and me; that makes eighteen. They were supposed to send us the transport today, but I've just heard back from my messenger. A real foul-up further north. You were right about west of here. There's a fast-moving Jerry column with Panzers going Hell-for-leather to the coast with nothing to stop them. To the east, there's another one, and to the south the French are holding back a third at Lille. At least they were holding them back but the situation is unclear now. The orders are to make for Dunkirk. I think the medical terminology is, we are in the shit!'

'So they're not sending transport?'

'Things are chaotic. We have to be ready to go at a moment's notice which is not easy with so many wounded. Oh, and Belgium has surrendered.'

'Shit! We'd better get a shift on, Major.'

'You're right, but we can't do anything until—if—the transport arrives. They are going to need pilots if Jerry tries to get across the channel. You'd better make a dash for the coast on your own. There's an army motorcycle out the back you could take.'

He's right. I could just go and leave everyone. 'You said there were sixteen soldiers to evacuate. How many are staying behind?'

The Doc gives me a long stare. 'I'm sorry, Harry. Only three. Your comrades, and another soldier who jumped on a grenade to save his pals. It blew out his guts and he won't last more than a couple of hours more. Poor lad has hung on now for forty-eight hours but the end is near. So we can't move him and to move your chaps is not in their best interests.'

I look around to make sure nobody is listening to our conversation. 'I didn't want to say anything earlier in case it spreads alarm. When I bailed out, a Jerry artillery spotter captured me. We came across a Waffen SS unit who had some British prisoners locked in a barn. I don't know how many. The SS murdered them.'

'Dear God!'

'The Jerry who bagged me let me go. He just let me go.'

'If we are still here when the Germans arrive we have to hope they are a disciplined unit. I've heard of the Waffen SS. They have a reputation for being ruthless.'

'Doc, I don't want to leave my friends here at their mercy.'

'I'm sorry, Harry, but moving them is too dangerous. It may kill them. You've done your bit, Harry. Best get yourself on your way to the coast. Use the motorbike before it's too late.'

'I'll hang on here for a while if you don't mind. See if I can help when your transport arrives.'

'All right, Harry, but don't let yourself get captured. You are needed in England.'

I go back upstairs and chat with Dickie. Larry is still asleep.

We have a laugh about a bar crawl through Rouen a couple of weeks ago when the gendarmes arrested us for being drunk and disorderly. Got a right roasting off the station commander but he couldn't afford to lose us. You can get away with a lot in war, it seems.

* * *

Dickie's tired, and Larry sleeps still, so I leave them and take a wander around the chateau grounds. The artillery in the distance rumbles on like a thunderstorm on the Mountains of Mourne, where I used to go camping as a child with my pals. It's funny how you get used to the sound of big guns. Well, funny is probably not the right word.

There's an orangery. All glass and full of tropical plants. I push the door open and go in. It's warm in here. I have no idea what all the foliage is, and I've never been to the tropics, but if it is anything like this, it's beautiful. I see huge flowers of pink and white. There's a pool in the middle of the orangery with some red-eared terrapins swimming around.

I breathe in the lovely scent that hangs in the air. It's so peaceful in here.

Over there by a rockery, on a bench, I can see the back of a soldier.

I duck under the low-hanging leaves of what may be a banana plant. 'Hello, don't stand up, didn't want to disturb you,' I say to the soldier's back.

He doesn't turn around.

I go round in front of him, but he still sits motionless.

He's young, about nineteen. A Fusilier according to his badges. The boy's eyes look red. I think he must have been crying.

'Are you all right?'

He just stares into space.

'What's wrong?'

Still no response. It's as if he is in a trance.

'Whatever it is, it can be sorted.'

His mind is away somewhere. He's like a shell on the beach at Ballycastle where Ma and Da would take us for a picnic. That's it, he's an empty shell. Where is the man inside? I'd better take him back to the chateau.

Gently, I put my hand under his arm and bring him to his feet. He makes no attempt to resist. As I lead him from the orangery, he walks as if ancient rather than nineteen. More of a shuffle really, than a walk.

I cross the gardens and come to the side door of the chateau.

'Paul, where 'ave you been? We 'ave been looking for you,' says a Red Cross nurse in the corridor as we enter. She's very different from Solange. I would put her in her fifties, with that matronly air about her.

'I found him in the orangery.'

'Merci.'

'What happened to him?'

'You must ask the Doctor.'

Major Driscoll comes down the back stairs. 'Ask the Doctor, what? Oh, there you are, Paul. Take him up to the ward please, nurse.'

She guides the young soldier up the stairs. He meekly complies with her instructions.

'I don't know what the psychiatric term is for what he has, Harry. I think it is something to do with him surviving an air raid. All his mates were killed, and he survived without a scratch. Some sort of guilt feeling. If I can get him back to England, he'll go to the psychiatric wing at Netley. They should help him there. We just can't get through to him.'

The Doctor heads off down the corridor leaving me to contemplate what I have just seen. There's Dickie with a broken body, Larry with a scorched face and lungs, and this young lad, Paul, who has abandoned his mind or it has abandoned him. This is war, and there is no glory in it. But I'm a fighter pilot and I have responsibilities to my country. I'm needed back in England.

* * *

At the back of the chateau, under a lean-to roof, I find a green-painted BSA M20. It's a beast of a machine with a 500cc engine. I used to have an old two-stroke BSA, but this one is a handful. Probably a dispatch rider's machine. I wonder what happened to him.

The petrol tank looks about half full. Yes, this should get me to the coast. I'm traveling light. Better see that this thing works first, though. I sit astride and pump the petrol lever. With my right foot, I press hard on the kick-start. There's a wheezing but no spark. I try again. Nearly. The third time the engine growls into tick over. I give it some revs. The noise in the lean-to is ear shattering. I cut the engine. The biggest problem will be trying to cross any rough ground. The clearance is very low, but I should be all right if I stick to the roads. I'll make my way north when I've helped the Doc load the patients, or as soon as I see Jerry coming this way.

I feel like a rat running out on Dickie and Larry but what can I do? Would Dickie or Larry run out on me? Only they know the answer to that question. I can't take them on the motorcycle, they can't walk, and the Doc won't take them. So I can't take them. That settles it. I have to leave them. What's the point of me staying and being captured too?

* * *

I make use of the sunny weather to explore the rest of the beautiful grounds. Red and white roses fill an oval garden next to a covered seating area on which I see a marble statue of Pandora, the first woman created by the gods. It's an ancient sculpture, not a reproduction. I've studied these and I know an original when I see one. Here, in this corner of Northern France, I find this jewel! I wonder who brought her here. I sit and enjoy looking at Pandora and the roses. An island of peace in a world of turmoil, with only the sound of buzzing bees in the flowers.

Much as I would like to, I can't stay here all day. I reluctantly rise to my feet. Maybe there are other hidden gems.

I come to a stable block. It looks older than the dressed, stone-built chateau. It is timber-framed and Elizabethan in style. I doubt the French would call it Elizabethan.

I push open the double door. Perhaps the Napoleonic soldier in the painting kept his white horse in this stable. Maybe the chatelaine had illicit liaisons in here. I sound like Jane Austen. Maybe not Austen, but perhaps one of those books you buy under the counter. There's only one horse, a dappled grey in a box with its head over the half door.

'Hello boy.'

'She's a mare.'

'Oh!' Solange is on the other side of the box.

'She's called Ursula.'

'That's an odd name for a horse.'

'Perhaps. She's named after Saint Ursula. Do you know the story of Saint Ursula? She was murdered because she would not submit to a man.'

'No, I'm a Protestant. We don't go in much for saints.'

'Is a pity.'

'That I am a Protestant or that she was killed?' Did I just say that?

Solange laughs. She has a wonderful smile.

'So, Mr. Fitzpatrick, er, Harry, when will you go?'

'I'm going to hang on until the transport gets here so I can help the Doc. Then I'll be on my way on the army motorcycle.'

'That must 'ave been the noise I heard. It frightened Ursula.'

'Sorry.'

'No need to be sorry, Harry. You go back to England?'

'I hope so.'

'I don't know what will happen here when the Germans come.'

Impulsively, I have an idea. 'Why don't you come with me on the motorcycle to the coast? They are evacuating the troops. They'll need nurses in England if France falls.'

Solange gives me a sad stare. 'You are very kind, Harry, but I could not leave my Papa here. And I have to look after your two friends and the other soldier.'

I nod. What can I say? I mustn't be selfish. Of course I'd love to ride the motorcycle up to the coast with Solange sitting behind me holding on round my waist. I can see she is very close to her father. And Larry and Dickie need her to look after them. I just hope nothing bad happens to her when the Germans come.

In the corner, I see a tarpaulin over a shape that could very well be a motor car. 'What's under there, if you don't mind me asking?'

Solange pulls the tarpaulin at one end to reveal a big Hispano-Suiza. I recognize the make from the badge on the front with the red cross and the silver stork mascot on the radiator grille. It isn't the latest model. I think it's a 1920s model, though it seems in good condition.

'This is Papa's. We used it when I travelled to horse shows. There's a horsebox that fits on the tow bar. Papa and I went all over France for the shows but we 'ave not 'ad any for a year due to the war. I don't know if the engine still works. It's been some time since we used it.'

'You used to compete?'

'Compete? Er, take part in the jumpings? Yes. I won some trophies. Do you ride, Harry?'

'Only a donkey at the beach.'

'I do not understand.'

'Sorry, just a joke. May I have a look in the car?'

'Yes.'

I pull open the heavy driver's door of the deep blue painted vehicle. The inside has brown leather bench seats in the front and a massive steering wheel on the left instead of the right. I think the best word to describe it would be luxurious.

'Impressive. Do you drive?'

'Oh yes. Papa taught me.'

The back has a well-upholstered bench seat. There's a wide gap between the back seats and the front seats. You could almost have a party in here, it's so big. The smell of leather gives it that extra air of splendour.

I close the door. 'So you drove the car all over France with your father? That must have been fun.'

'It was, 'arry. Papa has been very good to me since Maman died.'

'Oh, sorry about your mother.'

'She died when we were in Indo-China. Malaria. I was only ten.'

'That's so sad.'

'It is. She was the daughter of an English Earl. I never met 'er. he died in the Boer War. My grandmother was what you English call a black sheep, so I never met her either.'

'A colourful pedigree!'

She nods and smiles but it is a sad smile this time. 'So you see, my Papa looked after me. Now I must care for him. I could not leave Papa alone.'

'I understand.'

Around the corner, in this L-shaped stable, I see a horsebox trailer. 'Is this what you used to go to the shows?'

'No. Papa bought it last year because the one we 'ad was no longer working properly, too old. But we never 'ad the chance to use it because of the war.'

Are those engines outside I can hear? Not the Germans already. I hurry over to the stable doors and look outside. There are two trucks, and they're British. The Doc's evacuation can go ahead.

The soldier who brought me tea in bed this morning strides across the stable yard. 'Doc sent me looking for you, sir. His compliments to you, and would you present yourself in the yard? The evacuation transport has arrived, sir.'

'Yes, so I see. Thank you.'

He salutes. I'm not wearing headgear, so I do not return the salute, but I nod.

'Well, Harry, time to load the patients.' She strides out of the barn and into the chateau.

I find the Doc checking over the first truck. 'I thought we weren't expecting the transport to arrive today?'

The Doc shrugs. 'That's the army way, Harry.'

We load the stretcher cases in the first truck and the walking wounded in the second. Two nurses go with the first one, one of them leading Paul by the hand.

'Good luck, Harry. Get on that bike and go north before it's too late. The lad with the grenade injuries passed away. I'm leaving only your two friends behind. I'm so sorry, Harry.' The Doc shakes my hand and then climbs up into the cab of the first truck.

With a scraping of the yard gravel, the trucks move out. I watch them go and wonder if I should have gone with them. But I stand a better chance of making it on the motorbike. It's hard to leave Dickie and Larry here. I hope the Jerries look after them. And Solange? She'd best hide until the area is under the proper control of the German military authorities. I wouldn't trust those bastards in the SS.

* * *

I go upstairs to say my goodbyes to Dickie, and Larry if he's awake. He is sitting, propped up. At least I presume that is Larry. Can't see his face for bandages. Both his hands have dressings on them.

'Is that you, Larry?'

'Don't know. Can't see myself.' That's Larry's sense of humour.

I can't say something banal like, 'how are you,' so I mumble a 'hello.'

'Harry! Dickie said you were here. Glad you made it. I had a spot of bother.'

Yes, that's definitely Larry. 'You certainly did. Sorry.'

'I don't think I'll be bowling for a while. Seems the old lungs are affected too. The Doc said I couldn't go on the evacuation because it may kill me. I'll probably die in a POW camp. Sorry old chap, I really must stop this feeling sorry for myself. There are a lot of fellows worse off than me.'

'The Jerry doctors will look after you, Larry.' I say it with more hope than conviction.

Dickie reaches under his pillow, pulls out an envelope, and hands it to me.

'Please get this through to Mary, if you can, Harry.'

What can I say? I'm leaving him and Larry here at the mercy of the Germans. If it's the Waffen SS who get here first, I have no doubt they will kill them as they did the prisoners in the barn. If I stay here, at best, I'll be a POW or at worst, shot. I have to go. Staying would be stupid and would achieve nothing useful. And I owe it to my country to defend it as best I can. Owe it to my country? Is that right?

'Good luck, Dickie, Larry, I'm off shortly on a dispatch rider's motorcycle.'

'Get back in the air, Harry and give 'em hell!' says Larry.

I walk out of the room quickly before Dickie sees the tears welling up in my eyes. I can't help thinking of the times Dickie, Larry, and I have had back in England and here in France. We've watched each other's backs in the air, and we've played hard down on the ground. We are not just comrades. We are real friends.

I am abandoning them to save myself.

Am I a coward? Am I using the need to get back and fight as an excuse to run out on my friends?

* * *

In the hall, I find Solange with a distinguished looking gentleman.

'Flying Officer Harry Fitzpatrick, this is my father, 'Enri Chappelle.'

Monsieur Chappelle offers his hand. I shake it. 'Pleased to meet you, Mr. Fitzpatrick. You are not leaving with the Major and the other soldiers?'

'No, sir. I'm using the military motorbike. The Doc and the nurses can manage without me.'

'In that case, do you have time for some lunch before you leave? I'm afraid it will not be much. You are welcome to share it with Solange and I.'

I don't know how long it will be before I get another meal. And having lunch with the elegant Solange is an opportunity only a fool would miss. 'Thank you, sir. I would be delighted.'

The lunch is a lot more than I expected. Rabbit with dauphinoise potatoes. Delicious! We eat in the kitchen, just Solange, her father, and I. The other staff members have all gone home to their families to wait for the Germans to arrive. Solange is in sole charge of Larry and Dickie. They could not be in better hands.

'So, Harry, may I call you Harry?'

'Yes, please do, sir.'

'That accent, is it Northern Ireland?'

'It is, sir. Belfast.'

'I have never been to Ireland. Travelled all over the world but that is one place I have missed out on, I am afraid.'

'It's a beautiful but troubled place, sir.'

'So I hear.'

'May I compliment you on your orangery, sir? Quite a collection of plants.'

'Yes, I spent a great deal of my life in Indo-China and collected many specimens to go with those collected by my forebears. I had an excellent young gardener with an interest in the plants but unfortunately, he was mobilised at the outbreak of the war. My head gardener is rather old and lacks the interest in them that the young one had. Solange helps. She is very knowledgeable about such matters.'

'I love the quietness of the orangery,' says Solange. Her eyes seem to sparkle.

'It must be interesting being in the RAF. Is it a career or are you in just for the war?' says Henri Chappelle.

'I joined up before the war, after I left university.'

'University? What was your subject?' He pours another glass of wine for me. I see the label. It's a Chateau Margaux. For sure, I cannot claim to be a wine expert, but I know this particular one is very expensive because Dickie bought a bottle when we dined at the Ritz, at his expense of course. It cost more than a month's salary.

'My subject? The Classics. I've always been interested in Ancient Greece and Rome.'

'Really, I have an interest in Ancient Greece, too.'

'I saw a sculpture of Pandora in the garden. It is an original Greek one, I believe. Am I correct?'

'You are, Harry. My great grandfather brought it back. You British have the Elgin marbles and I have Pandora! Perhaps one day I shall return her to her home if the Greeks can be relied on to care for her properly.'

'If you don't mind me saying, sir, I think you had best hide Pandora. From what I have heard about the Germans in Poland and Norway, they have stolen any art treasures they can lay their hands on.'

'I'm afraid she is rather too heavy to be moved quickly and I fear the Germans will be here soon.'

'It would be a dreadful shame if Pandora ended up adorning some Nazi hall in Berlin.'

'Indeed.' He gives a Gallic shrug. 'Solange studied Mesopotamia at the Sorbonne. It seems you both have an interest in the ancient world.'

I look at Solange. She's smiling. Leaning back in her chair with a glass of wine in her hand, she asks me at which university I studied.

'Oxford.'

'Oxford? That is indeed the top one to study the Classics. Not at all easy to enter unless your family has connections.'

'I'm afraid, Solange, that my family does not have the right connections. I was fortunate.'

Henri Chappelle interjects. 'Have you any intention of taking your studies further, Harry?'

'Yes, indeed. When I have finished my time in the RAF, I am going to Greece. I shall become a world-famous archaeologist.' I laugh so I do not sound arrogant.

Monsieur Chappelle raises an eyebrow. 'An intriguing future. I wish you luck. Perhaps, if I still own Pandora when all this is over, I will ask you to take her home.'

'That would be an honour, sir.'

'Solange, tell Harry about your work.'

Solange takes a sip of her wine and smiles. Her teeth are as perfect as the rest of her. 'I studied Mesopotamia Civilisation at the Sorbonne. Then I worked as a researcher at the Louvre to finish my studies. Someday, I shall travel to Iraq and Syria and visit the sites that I have read so much about.'

I can see her father is very proud of his daughter's achievements. They clearly have wealth, but that has not spoiled her. On the contrary, she was a competitive horsewoman, a historian, and now a nurse.

'But you are a nurse now instead of a researcher.'

'I am, Harry. I used to come home from Paris whenever I could, and we would go to the horse shows. When war was declared, I decided to return 'ome permanently and train as a nurse to help our soldiers. I didn't want to stay in Paris. I missed Papa.'

Her father shuffles on his chair. 'And I was glad to have you come home. I'm worried now about the future. What do you think, Harry? Is it all over for France?'

'I don't know, sir. It doesn't look good. Some of the French and British armies are boxed up like kippers, so there is little chance of a breakout. But your army is still holding the Maginot line, as far as I know, to stop the Germans getting to Paris.'

'Huh! The Maginot line. What a waste of money that has proved.'

'You're not beaten yet.' Though I say it, I do not believe it.

'In the last war, we held them but at great cost. This time they just bypass our defences and come through Belgium where of course the Maginot line stopped.'

'Papa was at Verdun.'

'That was hell on earth, sir, I believe.'

'It was, Harry. It is with great sadness that I say this, but it may be better for us all that the Germans have managed to defeat us so quickly. We could not have years of carnage like the last war.'

'Papa, France must never give in. We must go on fighting. We are not finished yet, Papa.'

'No, Solange. A wise man knows when he is defeated.'

'I don't know how long Britain will hold out after this, sir.'

'Long enough for the Americans to join in I hope. They made a difference in 1917, but that was after three years of war. I doubt the British can hold out for three years this time.'

'Well, sir, we have the Canadians, Australians, Kiwis and the rest of the Empire. We also have many Poles and Czechs in the RAF. We even have a few Americans who have decided to fight the fascists. We are not done for yet.'

'I agree, Harry. Papa, we must not give in.'

Her father smiles and shrugs.

The sound of running feet on tiles makes us all

look over to the door. A short, wiry man with a huge moustache bursts into the kitchen.

He says something in rapid French that I can't understand. From his agitated appearance, I guess it isn't good news.

Solange puts her hand to her mouth as she gasps.

Her father stands up. 'Harry, you must go, quickly. Pierre says there's a column of Germans heading in this direction. He says they are an SS division and have been responsible for some terrible crimes. Go, Harry, go! Solange, I want you to go with him. It is not safe for you to stay here.'

Solange answers him in French. Though I cannot translate, I can tell she is refusing to go.

'Your father is right. I didn't want to alarm, but the SS murdered a barn full of British soldiers a couple of days ago. They will shoot Dickie and Larry. I have no means of saving them, but if they capture you, it will be—'

'I cannot leave my Papa!'

'I have an idea that may save your friends and Solange. Come with me, Harry.'

CHAPTER THREE

Solange sits in the driver's seat of the Hispano-Suiza, revving the engine to make sure it does not stall after the trouble we had to get it started. She's wearing her nurse's uniform and has packed a small suitcase. I have only the clothes upon my back.

Black smoke billows from the exhaust; I'm hoping that it's from little use rather than serious problems. Her tears fall like summer rain. They make my eyes water, too. She has put her duty as a nurse before that of a daughter, and it is churning her insides. The horsebox, with Larry and Dickie inside on stretchers, attached to the car's tow bar. Luckily, it's clean enough to use for the wounded. We're all set. It will not be an easy journey. Am I risking their lives? Probably. I think it is less of a risk than leaving them.

The Germans are close. The man who brought the news is keeping watch from the roof of the chateau. He's calling down to Monsieur Chappelle. From his agitation, I think he can see the Jerries. We have to go, quickly.

'Go, Harry, go. They're nearly here.'

I shake Monsieur Chappelle's hand. 'Thank you, sir. Please keep yourself safe.'

'Thank you, Harry. Look after Solange. Now go.'

'Will you not come with us, sir?'

'No, Harry. My place is here. God speed.'

I would stand a better chance on the military motorcycle just looking out for myself. Sometimes you have to look out for others. I couldn't leave Dickie and Larry. Solange is coming in her own right as a nurse, not as a passenger. We will need her.

Solange jumps out of the car and throws her arms around her father. It's making me well up even more. He extricates himself from her. She climbs into the horsebox.

I climb into the driver's seat and press my right foot hard on the accelerator. Away we go. Dickie and Larry may not survive the journey, but they had the choice of staying. It did not surprise me that they were willing to take the risk of trying for the coast.

Hell! I can see soldiers running across the fields from my right. They are about fifty yards ahead of us. Definitely German. I can make out six. Maybe more hide in the long grass. We haven't even started yet, and it looks as if it is already over.

They open fire from the field. I hear a couple of hits on the side of the car. God! I hope none hit the horsebox. Should I pull over and surrender?

Two soldiers dash out into the road. One has a Schmeisser levelled at the car and the other a rifle. They're Waffen SS. I can tell from their forage caps and black uniforms. There's no way I'm stopping for them. They'll shoot all of us.

I press the accelerator to the floor. With the horsebox attached, I can't pick up much speed quickly, and I'm worried about shaking Dickie and Larry up.

The soldier with the Schmeisser opens fire. The weapon kicks up. I can see he's a youngster. He's only about ten yards up ahead. Probably fresh out of the Hitler Youth and not used to the weapon or it wouldn't have kicked up. Maybe he's purloined it from a dead or wounded comrade. However he came by it, thank God he doesn't know how to use it.

The soldier with the rifle dives out of the way. I see the face of the other turn to panic and then fear. He's some mother's son, and he's only a teenager. He freezes. I can't swerve, or I may overturn the horsebox. I strike him hard with the front of the Hispano-Suiza. We're only doing forty kilometres to the hour according to the gauge. It's enough to knock him down. I feel a bump as the back wheels go over him. If he isn't dead, the war is over for him Squashed like a hedgehog.

I can't see anything in the rear-view mirror other than the horsebox. Stupid young man. I'm not going to lose much sleep over him though. He was out to kill us. With my heart beating like the wings of a hummingbird, I drive on.

Once out of the chateau's grounds on the road to the coast, we run into columns of fleeing refugees on bicycles, horse and carts, old motor cars, and on foot. I feel we have let these people down. I don't know if the Jerries will come after us. Their Panzers will cut across the fields and get ahead of us. A feeling of dread seeps up from my stomach to my throat. God help us!

At the first patch of open ground where I can pull over, I stop and jump out of the car. I have to see if those in the horsebox were injured.

I see daylight through three holes in the side of the box, up high.

To my relief, as I climb in, Dickie raises himself on his elbow. 'That was good of them. It was getting a little stuffy in here.'

Solange sits on the floor. I can see the fear in her eyes. Perhaps she can see the same in mine.

'We are all right, Harry. Don't worry.'

I wish I could agree with her.

* * *

At this rate, the Jerries shall overtake us. What would be our fate then? There are a few British and French soldiers among the refugees. A beaten army; I can see it in their faces. Most of them have discarded their rifles and packs and move with bowed heads.

A heavily-laden cart pulled by a tired old nag takes up most of the road. I can't get past. The Jerries can't be far behind. A blast on the horn does not elicit a response from the driver whom I am unable to see for the mattress and piano on the cart. Silly old bugger. We crawl along for nearly an hour, the driver oblivious to my horn. I feel sweat run down the back of my neck. Jerry's Panzers could appear at any time. Phew! At last, the road widens out. I squeeze the Hispano-Suiza past.

Upon the driver's seat of the cart, I see an old man, an old woman, and two children. Perhaps their grandchildren. Why take a piano? I doubt they were able to load it themselves. It's strange what people want to save when disaster strikes.

I keep my eyes peeled on the fields both sides of the road. Panzers could come our way at any time.

I see a JU 88 flying low over the road and coming directly for us from my left. On the seat next to me is Dickie's .38 Webley but it is of no use against a fighter plane; I discovered that when I bailed out. The people on the road dive into the ditches. The plane is so low I can see the swastika on the tail. I expect a stream of cannon fire. It doesn't come. The plane lifts as it nears our vehicle. Perhaps the pilot has some compassion. He would have killed many women and children had he fired.

No, it wasn't compassion; he has a mission.

It's heading for a clump of trees way off to my right. I see a black plume of smoke and debris shoot up into the sky. The Junkers pilot must have hit a British emplacement. I can't help whoever was under that bomb. They called this war a phony war since last September. For the last couple of weeks, it has been all too real.

With the JU 88 gone, the refugees climb out of the ditches and continue on their way. A sorry stream of people as far as the eye can see carry only what they could salvage. Nobody heads for the carnage left behind by the Junkers. Is it really every man for himself? God, I hope not.

Ahead I can see a small group of soldiers sitting on the roadside. They have no rifles. I can't see their packs. Perhaps they have just given up. As I drive slowly past, one of them springs onto the running board on the passenger side. I have the window open for fresh air.

'Stop the bloody car. We're having it,' demands a West Country accent.

With my left hand on the steering wheel, I make a grab for the Webley. 'Get off or I'll blow a hole in you.'

The soldier makes a grab through the window at the pistol. I don't want to shoot him. With a hard down-swipe, I hit him across the back of the hand with the barrel.

'Bastard!' he yelps. He jumps off holding his knuckles. I may have cracked some of them. Cretin!

This is turning into a nightmare. Where is the discipline? Surely, the army couldn't have just collapsed into a rabble.

Later I see a unit of around company size in kilts. They have packs on their backs and sloped rifles as they march in step three deep along the road with a piper playing out in front. God Bless 'em! The refugees part like the Red Sea as the soldiers come through.

Down the ages men marching Alexander, Caesar, and Napoleon led their men to their deaths. At least they led them. These days they lead from way back. Why do we let them do it?

The monotony of the drive at this pace is wearying. Twice I've nearly run off the road. Soon I'll have to stop for a rest, or we won't make it much further. If I stop, chances are some of our soldiers will try to steal the car. This is a nightmare journey. It would have been much easier to go on the motorcycle. I hate to admit this, but I am beginning to wish I had. That must be a sign of how low I too have sunk. Don't give in Harry. You owe it to Dickie, Larry, and Solange too. Get them through.

I haven't checked the dials for ages. I glance down. The needle for the temperature is way over in the red. I'm not an engineer, but I know that is not good. I see steam rising from under the bonnet. That's all we need! Damn. We can't carry Dickie and Larry all the way to the coast. And I can't leave them here.

All this low gear travel has taken its toll on the engine. I pull over to the side of the road.

Solange comes out of the back of the horsebox. 'What is wrong, Harry? Why 'ave we stopped?'

'Don't know. Overheating.'

'Can you make it work?'

'I don't know much about car engines, Solange. I'll have to have a look. How are Dickie and Larry?'

'The bumpy road is not good for them, Harry. They are fine for now, but I do not know 'ow much longer they can bear this.'

'If I can't fix the engine they won't be suffering the road anymore.'

I lift the bonnet. Steam hisses from a black hose attached to the radiator. Damn!

In the car's boot, I rummage around in the forlorn hope that there may be a spare hose. There's a toolbox but no hose. How am I going to fix it? I have no idea. We've been travelling for hours and haven't gone more than a few miles. We can't carry Dickie and Larry. They would have been better off if I had left them at the chateau.

'It's no good, Harry?'

'No good, Solange. I can't repair it, and I doubt there is a garage nearby willing to have a look.'

I'm a member of the Automobile Association in the UK. This is one place we won't see their motor-bikes and sidecars. All I need is a hose, but I may as well wish for the moon. I sit on the driver's seat with my feet out of the door, resting on the roadside verge.

Solange peers into the engine and shrugs. She's a talented woman, but I doubt she is a car mechanic.

'What do we do now, 'Arry?'

'I've no idea, Solange. If you join the queues making their way north, you may be lucky enough for the army to allow you to go to England. They need nurses.'

'What are you going to do?'

'I'll stay here to look after Dickie and Larry.'

With a heavy heart, I step into the horsebox. From my face, it is evident Dickie knows there is bad news coming. 'Sorry, Dickie, Larry, the game's up. A hose has gone, and there's no chance of replacing it. I've asked Solange to go on ahead. I'll stay here with you until the Germans catch up with us. Hopefully, we will be sent to the same POW camp.'

'Harry,' says Larry. 'You've done all you can for us. And I thank you for that. But you must go on ahead. Don't get bagged with us. You can escape and give the blighters some grief. Save yourself, Harry, and Solange, too.' His voice sounds faint.

I don't think he's going to make it. I shake my head. I step out of the horsebox to think.

The fields all around are full of wheat and hay. Overhead I can see a kite enjoying a thermal. Apart from the pathetic lines of humanity fleeing the Germans, it is a rural paradise here. Will this be my last resting place? If it is, then it is a fine place to spend eternity. I need a miracle.

Don't give up, Harry, I tell myself. Leaving them to the mercy of the Germans while I escape is not an option. Solange must go on. If I can persuade some soldiers to help me carry them—

'What's up, mate?'

I turn to see a British soldier. He's a short fellow with a ruddy complexion and no hat on his ginger hair. His uniform would incur the wrath of his sergeant major due to its creases and dirt. He has kept his rifle and pack which is a sign that at least he hasn't given up. As I have taken off my flying jacket and my uniform jacket, he would be oblivious to the fact that I am an officer.

'Overheating.' I shake my head.

'All right, mate. Jimmy James, RASC and don't joke about it standing for 'run away, somebody's coming,' because I've had enough of that. Tell you what I'll do. I'll fix it for you if you give me a lift.'

'If you fix it, you get your ride.' Is he the miracle?

Jimmy James hands me his rifle and slips off his pack. For nearly an hour, he has his head inside the bonnet clanging, banging, and waving a screwdriver from the toolbox. The fleeing refugees don't even stop to look. It seems curiosity dies with hope.

Solange keeps checking on the two patients in the horsebox and gives them a running commentary on the progress. She hasn't said anything but I can tell from the look on her face that she's worried about Larry.

'Right, mate, run the engine.'

I climb into the driver's seat and start the car. Jimmy James peers into the engine compartment. After five minutes, he slams down the bonnet and sticks up a thumb.

'You managed to fix it!'

'Yeah, no problem mate. Shortened one hose and used the extra for the repair.'

'You've earned your ride, Jimmy James. Get in.'

'Who you got in the back with that bint?'

'A couple of wounded airmen. And she's a nurse, not a bint.'

'Oh, no offence, mate.'

Jimmy climbs into the front passenger seat. He lifts the Webley to put it on the back seat where I left my uniform jacket and his rifle and pack. I can't help smiling at his expression when he sees the two black bands on the sleeve signifying that the owner is an RAF Officer.

'Oops, sorry, sir!'

'Don't worry about it, Jimmy. Glad to have you aboard.'

We carry on along the road to the coast, but the crowds become even thicker. In the last couple of hours, I've seen a lot more soldiers making their way north. Some are in good order marching along with their rifles and packs. I even passed a Welsh battalion, singing.

It's getting dark and to carry on would be dangerous with so many people. I see a barn just a little way off the road, up a track. As gently as I can, to spare Dickie and Larry the pain, I steer the car and pull up outside the barn. It's derelict with a collapsing roof, but it will do for tonight. Nobody else seems to be here so we will have it to ourselves.

On Solange's advice, we leave Dickie and Larry in the horsebox. She changes Larry's dressings. I can hardly look at the poor fellow. I'm not sure I would want to survive if I was in his state. But then, life is precious, and perhaps I would fight to keep going. Larry certainly is not a quitter.

Monsieur Chappelle's generosity extended further than the gift of his car and horsebox. We have two bottles of wine, bread, cheese, slices of ham and some cold rabbit. Solange shares the food with Larry and Dickie. She has to feed Larry.

Jimmy, Solange, and I then sit down inside the barn to eat our share. The wine is a passable Burgundy.

'So what happened to you then, Jimmy?'

'Buggered if I know, sir. My unit followed the retreat trying to keep all the vehicles on the road. Somehow, I was separated and decided to head for the coast with the rest of the rabble. It's a SNAFU and no mistake if you don't mind me saying, sir.'

'What is this SNAFU?' Solange inquires.

'Situation Normal All er… Up,' I say.

She looks at me for a moment and then bursts into giggles. Her English colloquialisms are clearly excellent.

Jimmy wanders off into a corner and beds down for the night.

Solange and I finish off the Burgundy.

'So, what are your plans when it is all over, Solange?'

'I do not know, Harry. I want to go 'ome and see my Papa. When will it be over? We do not know, and what is over? What will the world be like when the Nazis rule it? I think they will. But we must fight on.'

'If we can cross to England, will you work as a nurse?'

'If they will have me, Harry, I will work as a nurse. I do not want to go to England but I must. It makes me very sad, Harry, to leave my Papa.'

'I understand that, Solange. These are dreadful times we live in.' I want to take her in my arms and hug her tightly; she seems so vulnerable tonight. That would be stupid of me to risk scaring her. She's mentally strong, I can tell, but she's scared and alone. To be honest, so am I.

'I will stay awake with your comrades tonight. You must sleep so you can drive tomorrow.' She stands and heads for the horsebox. I do not stop her. This is not the time and place for anything other than getting all of us to England.

* * *

Wednesday 29th May 1940

I wake feeling cold and stiff. Through the missing barn door, I see Jimmy checking over the Hispano-Suiza. The sound of artillery to the south of us carries on the still morning air. How far away, I am unable to tell, but it seems too close. We must press on. I can see across the fields to the road, and already a trail of fleeing refugees and soldiers tramp northwards.

'Sorry, Harry.' Solange steps out of the horsebox. She looks drained and exhausted. 'I am so sorry. Larry died in the night I think his heart just gave out. I did not want to disturb you. It will be a long day's drive.'

Guilt hits me in the chest like an assegai. Why did I not leave the poor chap in the chateau? He may have survived. I don't say anything, sit on the ground, and cover my face with my hands.

'Don't blame yourself, Harry. You tried to help your friend. It was his decision to come. He did not have to.'

She's right, but it still hurts.

In the barn, I find a spade. It's rusty but sound. With Jimmy's help, I dig a grave. How many men are we leaving behind in the earth? So many men lie in graves here from the 1914 and 1918 conflict. You would think we would have enough sense in Europe not to do all this again. But perhaps this is one war that we must fight. Hitler must be stopped, but by whom? France is about to fall, and I have a dreadful feeling that Britain won't last much longer.

With Jimmy holding his feet and me under his arms, we lay Larry in the patch of ground. The words of Rupert Brooke come into my head.

If I should die, think only this of me;

That there's some corner of a foreign field

That is forever England.

For me, it will be Ireland.

Dickie watches from his stretcher Please God, don't let him die too.

We have no shroud or coffin. Larry lies wrapped in a sheet. I say a few words that seem meaningless to me and then the Lord's Prayer. We cover him and I mark the grave's site on my map. If I make it back to England, I will tell his parents where he lies and the authorities so they can give him a proper burial at some time in the future when the world is free; if that ever happens.

I've spent my university years and those after studying the ancient world and their lives. I wonder what someone will make of today's time if archaeologists in a couple of thousand years excavate this area. What will we leave behind about us? Will they think us fools? Perhaps by then, wars will be unheard of though I suspect we humans have the capacity to keep on killing each other ad infinitum.

I sit down on the ground next to Dickie. 'I'm sorry. I should have left you at the chateau.'

'No, Harry. Larry made his decision. He would not have lasted long in a POW camp. Keep going, Harry. I'm relying on you to get me back to England. Do you still have that letter I gave you?'

'Yes.' I pull it from my pocket and place it on his blanket.

'Thanks, Harry. I'll deliver it myself! But if anything should happen—'

'I will, Dickie. I promise.'

Silence pervades the field in which poor Larry lies. The trees in the nearby wood seem to harbour only malevolence. Lines I learned at school from Shakespeare's Sonnet about age flits into my mind and I speak them softly to Dickie.

That time of year thou mayst in me behold
When yellow leaves, or none, or few, do hang
Upon those boughs which shake against the cold,
Bare ruined choirs, where late the sweet birds sang.
In me thou see'st the twilight of such day
As after sunset fadeth in the west;
Which by and by black night doth take away,

Death's second self, that seals up all in rest.
In me thou see'st the glowing of such fire,
That on the ashes of his youth doth lie,
As the death-bed, whereon it must expire,
Consumed with that which it was nourish'd by.
This thou perceiv'st, which makes thy love more strong,
To love that well, which thou must leave ere long.

Dickie reaches up and puts his hand on my arm. We were once jolly young men with all our lives in front of us. Now we sit here, Dickie physically broken and my mind in danger of going like that of young soldier Paul back at the chateau.

I must pull myself together or we shall all perish.

We leave and head north. Solange sleeps on the back seat and Jimmy is in the horsebox with Dickie. I hope we don't lose Dickie too. A heavy sense of foreboding hangs over me. I feel so weary. How can I kick this air of depression?

We've been trundling along now for about four hours and have only travelled a few miles. There's artillery fire coming from ahead of us, whistling over towards the south. That must be British or French guns. I hope they know where their shells are landing because there are people as far back as you can see along the road and some in the fields.

Though camouflaged, there are machine gun posts and trenches off to both sides of the road.

It looks as if this is where what is left of our army is going to make a stand. God help them. There is no way of knowing what the plan is, if there is one. I just hope they can hold back the Germans long enough so as many of us as possible escape.

It's late evening. The sun turns the sky in the west into a spectrum of orange and red. Most appropriate for what is happening across this country. I can smell newly-mown hay. It reminds me of home. Not that there was much haymaking in the Shankill, but when we went out to the countryside for picnics on the charabanc we ran around the fields and played in the haystacks. Looking back now, I think Ma and Da chose the days of the Orange Order marches to leave Belfast. Strange now, looking back. They were staunch Protestants, my parents, but they never took part in any of the marches. This evening the sky is orange. I don't think that is symbolic. My mind is wandering. I must keep my concentration going. My eyes are heavy. We shall have to stop soon.

Now there's a roadblock with British soldiers checking refugees and sending them off down a path to the left. The road ahead leads to Dunkirk. They must be trying to keep the evacuation route clear. More orderly units march with their rifles and packs towards the coast. There's a battalion of Sikhs ahead, striding out in perfect formation.

The fuel gauge is low due to the crawling speed.

I pull off the road to see if Jimmy can do something.

Solange, asleep on the back seat, wakes when the soporific motion of the vehicle stops.

'Problem, Harry?'

'We're low on fuel.'

Jimmy checks the gauge. 'Yeah. We're in trouble. We'll be lucky to get another hour out of it at this pace.'

I see some flashes in a wood over to my right. That's an artillery position. They may have some fuel we can use.

We stop at the roadblock. A young lieutenant comes to the driver's window. 'Who are you?'

'Flying Officer Fitzpatrick. I have a Flight Lieutenant in the horsebox. He's severely injured. We need to get through, but we're short on fuel. Any chance you could let us have some?'

The lieutenant shakes his head. 'No, no chance. We don't have any transport. Looks like we're the last-ditch stand. Off to the right. Try down there. It's the Royal Artillery; they have some transport though I don't know if they'll let you have any. Good luck.'

The lieutenant waves us through the roadblock. I drive along a track to the artillery emplacement. For an army on the retreat, they look professional and well-organised. They have tents in the woods, ammunition stacked behind sandbags, and three 4.5-inch guns in almost constant use.

Three AEC artillery tractors lie under a camouflage net.

Unlike the German half-tracks and 88s, these chaps are dug in for a last stand, not movement. The noise is deafening.

A sentry with a rifle stops us. I've put my uniform jacket on so they know who I am.

'Yes? Sir.'

'We need some fuel to make it to the coast. I was hoping you could let us have some.'

'Pull up over there, sir.' He points to a patch of clear ground big enough to take the Hispano-Suiza and the horsebox.

The whiff of cordite fills the air. Somewhere mixed in there with it is the scent of some wild flowers at the side of the emplacement. I'm not a gardener or florist and have no idea what they are, but they are a welcome addition to cordite.

A lance bombardier marches over to the car. He salutes as if he's on the barracks square in Aldershot.

I acknowledge with a nod as I am without headgear. 'Any chance of some fuel?'

'Please wait here, sir.'

The lance-bombardier marches off to a tent and comes back with a major.

'You want fuel?' says the major. He's a tall man with sandy hair and moustache to match. His accent is Home Counties hunting set.

'I have an injured pilot in the horsebox. We're trying to get to the coast.'

Solange steps out of the car. The major raises an eyebrow.

'This is Solange. The car is her father's. She's a nurse, helping me with the patient.'

'It's getting dark. You'd best stay here until first light. I can let you have a little fuel but on one condition.'

I don't like the sound of that. 'What condition?'

'Two of my lads are badly hurt. I want to evacuate them, but I can't spare anyone. You take them, and you can have the fuel.'

'Fair enough.' Well, we don't have much choice other than to take them. If we don't we don't get the fuel. I hope they aren't too badly injured or Solange may not cope.

The big guns fall silent as the night creeps in. The major has given us a tent. Jimmy and I carry Dickie inside. The four of us will have to make do in here.

A soldier brings us some rations. Some bully beef and beans but it's enough. Dickie manages to help himself to his food. Solange, Jimmy, and I sit cross-legged on the ground and eat ours.

The major comes in with a bottle of whisky and some tin mugs. He hands them around to Solange, Dickie, me, and Jimmy and keeps one for himself. I can see Jimmy is embarrassed to be drinking with officers.

The major has noticed this too. 'Don't worry. This isn't the officers' mess. So, Fitzpatrick, what's your story?'

'Dickie and I were shot down back there. Solange's father has given us his car to get to the coast. What are your orders?' I know he might not be able to share, but I ask anyway. Can't hurt.

'We're to hold the German advance for as long as possible, while our chaps are evacuated from Dunkirk.'

'You've been shelling all day. You know where the Germans are?'

'Yes. They're holding up a few miles south of here. I don't know why they don't just keep coming. If they do, they'll go through us like a knife through butter though I hope we'll give a good account of ourselves.'

'When are you going to evacuate?'

He shakes his head and takes a slug of the whisky. 'We're not. We're to hold out for as long as possible. They said the French would relieve us but I doubt that will happen. They're up to their armpits in Panzers down near Lille and over at Abbeyville from what I heard.'

'Apparently, one German column is already on the coast west of here.' I say.

'I know. But it seems they have halted their advance throughout this sector. We're part of a perimeter ring to keep Dunkirk operational. It seems that someone somewhere has a plan. I wish they'd had a decent one before this cock-up. You'd best be on your way at first light. I'll have my two chaps ready.'

I finish my whisky. It has helped to drive away

most of the melancholy from worrying about what I will have to tell Larry's parents, if I manage to get back to England. I pray this lift in my spirits is not just a temporary alcoholic relief.

'Thanks for your hospitality, major,' says Dickie, taking a sip of his whisky.

He's coping well with the rigours of this trip. I just hope I can get him back to England, alive. Dickie is an inspiration and it is watching him cope that gives me the strength to keep going. I know that if the situation were reversed, with me injured and him in charge of getting us away, he would not fail. I must hang on to that.

Keep going. Don't give up.

The major leaves us. We bed down for the night.

The face of the young SS soldier I killed with the Hispano-Suiza flashes in front of me. The bump as the wheel runs over him shakes me. I sit up and open my eyes. A dream. My shirt sticks to my skin with sweat. He was trying to kill us so why do I feel bad about running him over? Strange. It's his face. So young. He could barely be out of school and yet they've made him into a killer. I suppose our side will be conscripting youngsters soon.

Solange wakes. 'What is it, 'Arry?'

'Just a dream, Solange. Go back to sleep.'

I lie down again to try to get back to sleep, but I can't. That face troubles me.

Thursday 30th May 1940

I come out of the tent into the damp early morning. Dew lingers on spiders' webs. Robert the Bruce may have taken inspiration from watching a spider try and try again to build its web, but I do not think the British army will copy him. It seems that defeat has already overtaken us. Can we stop the Germans on the beaches of England? First, they have to cross the Channel against the Royal Navy and then, I hope, we have enough planes left to gain air superiority and soldiers to fight them.

After some sleep, I feel more optimistic. Just that feeling of optimism has given me a boost. Maybe it isn't all over. Today, I feel more positive about our fate.

The scent of flowers and damp leaves has taken the upper hand.

Somewhere out in the wood, I hear a cockerel crowing. There must be a smallholding or farm nearby, perhaps with someone like Mariette in residence. I smile when I think of her. It's these sounds and smells of normality that makes it all so surreal.

The major strides over to me. 'Come with me, Fitzpatrick, and bring your nurse.'

I step back into the tent. Solange is up and doing her best to make herself presentable. Even though she is unable to wash or change her clothes, her elegance remains. There's definitely something about her that is getting to me. I don't know, she's very attractive and clever and she's a historian like me but it's more than that. Something she exudes from deep within her. I wish I could get to know her better.

I beckon her to come with me.

The three of us make our way through the artillery camp, careful not to fall into any of the many foxholes that may become the graves of these poor fellows. We come to a tent set back from the guns. The major lifts the flap. We follow him in.

Two soldiers lie on camp beds. I can see one has his eyes bandaged and the other has lost a leg.

The major turns to Solange. 'Could you see what you can do for them? We don't have a medic, but one of my chaps has done his best for them.'

Solange checks the amputee. Her nimble fingers remove the bandages. She turns her head as the smell of gangrene permeates the tent. I have to stop myself from retching. Solange says nothing, turns back to the patient and covers the awful sight with a piece of cloth.

She unwinds the bandage round the other soldier's eyes to reveal burn marks.

'Can you take them? Look, I'm not a complete bastard. I want the best for them so if you think moving them will be too much then say so and I'll still let you have the fuel.' I can see the major feels deeply for his men. He's old school military but with a heart as big as they come.

Solange steps away from the patients and makes her way outside. We come out after her.

'The one with the burns we can take. He's blind, and it will probably be permanent. The other, gangrene has set in. I'm not a doctor, and he needs one soon. I'll clean up 'is wound. It's a risk to move him, but if he doesn't get to a doctor, then he's going to die.'

The major nods.

'Get Jimmy to help me,' says Solange.

'I'll help you,' I say.

'Thank you, Harry but I think Jimmy will be of more use.'

I'll say one thing for Solange, she's direct. I fetch Jimmy and leave them to do whatever she has planned. Should I feel a tinge of jealousy? Perhaps but funnily enough I don't. She's professional and I have to stay that way too.

The major instructs one of his men to fill the Hispano-Suiza's tank from a petrol can.

Two hours later, with the guns firing again, Solange and Jimmy come out of the hospital tent.

'We're ready to load them now. Put Dickie in first.' Solange looks tired.

With the help of the major's team, we load Dickie and the two wounded men on stretchers into the horsebox. Jimmy sits in with them. Solange joins me in the car.

The memory of laying Larry in his grave worms its way into my brain. The guilt piles up inside me. I can't help this feeling of utter helplessness. I'm all right up in the blue on my own. Down here there are too many people relying on me and so far I've failed Larry. Will I fail all of them?

Through the open window, I offer my hand to the major. 'Thank you.'

He nods. 'Good luck, Fitzpatrick. I have a letter here. Would you be so kind as to make sure my wife sees it if you make it back home? The address is on the envelope. I know the post should go through the proper channels, but those channels do not seem to exist now.'

It's the least I can do for the man. As he passes me the envelope, I see the address is in Reigate in Surrey. Small world. Dickie lives in Reigate. I hope he can deliver his own letter.

I wonder what will happen to the men we are leaving behind. If not killed in the action, then they will surely become POWs, unless the SS decide to shoot them. Should I have told the major about my experience with the SS? I don't know. It didn't seem right to add to his troubles.

CHAPTER FOUR

We're only two miles from Dunkirk now. The last part of the journey has gone faster due to fewer refugees clogging up the roads. As we pass through the villages, I see the houses shuttered as if they could keep out the approaching nightmare. What will life be like for these people under the yoke of the Nazis? The German artillery spotter reminded me that not all the enemy are monsters, but my encounter with the SS proves that there are enough of them to make this country recoil from their barbarism.

The remaining refugees still make their way to the coast but with the roadblocks sending them off in all directions, the way through is less torturous. Every few hundred yards, I see men dug into defensive positions and families crossing in front of them. If it wasn't for the dire circumstances, it could be a comic opera.

I pull over to the side of the road. It's three hours since we left the artillery emplacement and our patients probably need some food, drink and a comfort break. We have only a little in the way of supplies. It is all the major could spare. I hope there is some more at Dunkirk.

Jimmy is a real brick, the way he's mucked in, helped with the injured, and kept the vehicle working. We would not have made it this far without him. I just wish I had the quiet confidence that seems to keep him going.

Solange dispenses water and deals with the delicate needs of our three invalids. It isn't the kind of work one expects a woman of her class to undertake even though she's a trained nurse.

Soon we are rolling on towards Dunkirk. Solange has taken Jimmy's place in the horsebox. He sits alongside me with his rifle.

'So, where are you from, Jimmy?'

'London, sir. Poplar.'

'Married?'

'Yeah, married Rosie seven years ago, now. Got a daughter, Lucy; she's five. Hope I get back to see them. I'm worried. If the Luftwaffe starts bombing…'

'I hope it doesn't come to that. You a career soldier?'

'Nah! I was working in the West India Docks, but it wasn't good. You never know how much work you're going to get. Sometimes I didn't work for weeks, and it's hard when you have a family. So, when Adolf started this war, I thought I'd join up before I was called up. The pay ain't too good, but it's regular. First time I've had a pay packet every week. I have to get home. I have to survive, or I don't know what will happen to Rosie and Lucy.'

'We'll make it, Jimmy.'

'What do you know about the new Prime Minister, Churchill, sir? I don't know much other than he was responsible for Gallipoli. My uncle was there. That was a SNAFU too.'

'I don't know more than you do, Jimmy. He's not popular in Wales due to trouble with the miners. We'll have to see. At least he's trying to extricate the army from the mess Chamberlain left behind. If he can hold us together to keep Jerry out, then we have to put our trust in him.'

'Well, maybe, sir. But he's a Tory⸺Look out!' Jimmy leaps out of the car with his rifle already aimed at the sky by the time he hits the ground.

I see a Junkers JU 88 coming in low from the right, all cannons blazing. Jimmy is down on one knee in front of the car firing at the Junkers. He has no chance of hitting it but I suppose it's worth a try. I don't think Jimmy is the quitting kind of fella. Soldiers return fire with rifles and Bren guns. The plane's shells spatter the road in front of me, only about ten feet in front and damned close to Jimmy. He's still firing. Bloody Hell! That's too close. Someone has hit the Junkers. Maybe it was Jimmy. Black smoke streams from the starboard engine. It's climbing.

Jimmy pokes his head through the open passenger window. 'Gawd love us!'

At the next roadblock, I reckon we're about half a mile from Dunkirk; a one-pip British lieutenant stops us.

'RAF? I say, shouldn't you be up there?' He points at the sky. 'Sorting out the Luftwaffe instead of running away?'

I feel the hairs on the back of my neck prickle. I know I'm tired and stressed, hungry and thirsty so I'm not in a good frame of mind. But if he doesn't watch his mouth, I'll have him by the throat.

He's every inch the Guardsman down to the cut glass accent. A tall chap no more than twenty with a sandy-coloured, wispy moustache, I've taken an instant dislike to him.

I take a couple of deep breaths. 'We're heading for Dunkirk, the evacuation. Is it still on?'

'What have you in the horsebox? I hope you haven't been looting. Capital offence, old boy.'

Now my fingers tingle on the steering wheel. Take deep breaths. That's better. 'Three wounded, old boy! Now get the fuck out of my way, we're going to Dunkirk.'

He blinks. I can see the broad Belfast accent coming from an RAF officer took him by surprise. The lieutenant calls over two soldiers with rifles. Both of them have bandages around their heads. They stand in front of the Hispano-Suiza. The lieutenant strides to the back of the horsebox. I jump out of the car and follow him. He pulls open the back doors.

Solange stands up and steps out of the horsebox. Dickie tries to sit up but lies flat again. The other two patients are asleep or dead.

'Civilians are not being evacuated. Some of the wounded may be, but they will have to take their turn. If they can't wade out to the ships, then they will not be able to go. So, I suggest you start walking in that direction, Miss.' He points back down the road we have just come from.

I step up close to the boy's face. 'She's coming with me. She's a nurse and I need her to look after my patients.'

'Thought you were a pilot, old boy, not a doctor. Makes no difference. Civilians aren't allowed. And the walking wounded are manning the defense line.'

'Listen, you ass, she's coming with me.'

He sniffs. His two soldiers blocking the road in front of the Hispano-Suiza have grins on their faces. I get the feeling that his military authority is hanging on by a thread. Why the hell have they left a boy in charge of this sector?

I've had enough, and it must show on my face because the boy suddenly steps to the side of the road. He seems to have had a loss of confidence.

'Just doing my job. On your way.'

Solange climbs back into the horsebox. Jimmy and I get into the car. I drive on.

As I pass one of the lieutenant's soldiers, he leans forward. 'Good luck, sir. Wish we were coming with you.' Poor sods. Left to hold the line because the brass failed completely.

We come across lines of men heading for the beaches. Jesus Christ! As we enter the town I see the damage. Buildings in ruins. Fires raging. Shell and bomb holes in the street. Unburied bodies. This place has taken one hell of a hammering. Stretching along the cratered beach are men huddled in groups. Some sit around fires. Offshore, I see several ships a fair way out. Lines of men up to their shoulders in the water wade out. Some carry rifles over their heads, but most have no weapons.

That sound. What is it? A Stuka. The scream of its siren fills the air and creates panic. I see men on the beach running for cover as it dives. The men in the sea break out of the line. What's it going for? That paddle steamer close in. The Stuka drops a bomb. It hits the water just to the side of the ship. A plume of water shoots up into the sky. Thank God it missed.

Shit! A second Stuka dives. He's heading for the same paddle steamer. There goes the bomb. It hits the steamer dead centre. The whole ship erupts in flames. Poor bastards. They don't stand a chance.

Small boats come shore and load up with men. Others make for the stricken paddle steamer. It looks chaotic. I think some of the small boats are ferrying the men out to the bigger ships where it's too deep to wade. The others won't find many survivors on the steamer.

Two ships lie moored at the harbour mole. This concrete finger that stretches from the harbour out to sea seems to point accusingly towards England and ask why we abandon France to her fate. Lines of men form up on the thin mole to board the ships in an orderly manner. We'll get off that way. We can't wade out to the other ships with our wounded.

I find space and stop the Hispano-Suiza. Almost immediately, a sergeant major from a Scottish regiment approaches me. He has a clipboard and a professional manner. 'Pilot?' he asks looking at my uniform.

'Yes.'

'Well, we've had precious little support from your lot down here but the powers that be say you have priority, sir. Leave the car there. Disable it and make your way to the mole. You see that naval officer at the beach end? He's in charge of the evacuation via the mole and will allocate you a place. With respect, jump to it, sir. We need to get everyone away as quickly as possible.'

'I have a wounded pilot and two wounded soldiers, and Jimmy here and a nurse to evacuate, too.'

'The injured pilot, can he walk?'

'No.'

'How bad is he?'

'He can't walk on his own.'

'Right then, sir. Please make your way to the mole. The others must remain on the beach. I hope they can get off, but they are not a priority.' He says something under his breath about the RAF but I can't quite make it out. I think it was an insult.

'I'm not leaving them.'

'Sir, with all due respect, you are needed in England. We have an evacuation plan to get as many able-bodied men off as possible. The others will have to take their chances. And with respect—let's just say, you'd better get aboard a ship soon because the chaps on the beach are not at all happy about the lack of support from your people.'

'Thank you, Sergeant-major.' What's the point of pulling rank? He's doing his best.

He strides away, leaving me unsure what to do now. I can't leave Dickie and Solange, or Jimmy. I don't want to leave the artillery lads either, but I'm the only one to have priority to board one of the ships. There's no way we can get stretchers through the surf to those smaller ships.

'Should we try somewhere else, sir?' Jimmy seems to sense my discomfort.

'This is it, Jimmy. There isn't anywhere else. And we may not have a chance here for long if the Germans decide to break through.'

'Then you'd better do what the Sergeant-major said, sir. Make your way to the mole. At least they'll let you board. I'll do what I can for Solange and the others.'

'I'm not leaving all of you here. Jimmy, you could join one of those lines wading out to the smaller ships and get away. You've got to get back for your family.'

'No, sir. I'm not leaving all of you. We've come this far together. Anyway, I can't bloody swim.'

'Well, until we sort something out, disable the car, and then we'll set up a base as best we can.'

Jimmy lifts the bonnet of the Hispano-Suiza and yanks out wires. Then he takes his rifle and whacks the fittings. Finally, he picks handfuls of sand and puts it in the engine through the oil filler.

'Need a bloody good mechanic to get this going again,' he says with a grin.

I feel sorry about the car. It got us here, and Solange's father was very fond of it. But I guess it is just another casualty of war.

Solange comes and stands by my side. The poor woman looks exhausted. 'It does not look good, Harry.'

'It doesn't, Solange. Don't worry. I won't leave you here.'

'I 'eard what that sergeant said. You can get away.'

I put my arm around her. The doubt and depression are under control, at last, and I know I shall not run out on my people. 'We all go, Solange, or none at all. How are Dickie and the other two?'

'They are all right, considering what they 'ave been through.'

'What's the best way to keep them comfortable? Should we keep them in the horsebox?'

'I think so.' She shrugs. I doubt she's able to come up with a better plan, given the circumstances.

With Jimmy's help, I unhitch the horsebox and push it into the shade of a ruined building. We make a little refuge between the horsebox and the wall where we lay Dickie and the two wounded artillerymen.

It's been a long day, and we've not eaten since breakfast. 'We need some food and drink. I have no idea how we will get any.'

'Leave it to me, sir.'

Jimmy is up on his feet and heading off into what is left of the town. There are so many soldiers milling around I fear he will be unsuccessful.

'Thanks for taking us, sir.' For the first time, I look properly at one of the wounded artillery soldiers. He's ginger and freckled with a Scots accent.

'How is it going?'

'I'm all right, sir.'

I look at Solange. She's behind him so he can't see her. She shakes her head. 'We need a doctor to check out that leg.'

I nod and set off along the beach to see if I can find one.

In the dunes, I find a small enclave with a Red Cross flag. Several soldiers lie on makeshift beds. Others just sit on the sand, nursing a range of injuries. Two soldiers with Red Cross armbands must be orderlies. A slim young man about my age tends to one of the wounded on a stretcher. From his shoulder markings, I see he's a captain.

I wait until he's finished tending the man on the bed. 'Are you a doctor?'

'Why?'

'I have three wounded men needing medical attention.'

'I have ten thousand needing attention.'

'Could you help me, please?' This is no time to get into an argument. 'I have a chap with gangrene.'

'Where?'

'Just over there, about a hundred yards.'

The doctor nods to one of his orderlies. 'Take over.' And then he turns to me. 'Come on then, I haven't got all day.' He grabs a Gladstone bag.

I take him to our enclave. Solange has undone the amputee's bandages and is washing the stump of his leg.

The doctor has a quick look at the injury. 'We'll have to improvise.' He turns to me. 'Go find some maggots. There's plenty around if you look for them.'

'Maggots?'

'Yes, maggots!'

I set off along the side streets, looking for a suitable maggot host. I find it slumped over a bottle of wine. He's been dead for a few days. The little white grubs have devoured most of his face. What little I had in my stomach is now on the ground.

Out at sea I hear that terrible scream of a Stuka dive-bomber but I can't see what he's going for due to the crumbling buildings.

Somewhere nearby I hear the pounding of artillery shells exploding. Welcome to Hell.

Discarded along with so much other rubbish and military equipment, I find an empty tin of beans. At arm's length, I scrape maggots from the body into the can and then throw up again. I don't know how many maggots the doctor wants but when I have the can half full I decide that will be enough.

Making my way back to the enclave, I see long lines of soldiers still heading for the beach. Most of them are in proper order, marching along in step. Between these units are gaggles of stragglers loping along.

They all scatter when three 109s come over, guns blazing. The street is littered with dead and dying.

I have to take care of my small party. Someone

else will have to deal with the other casualties. I run back to my enclave.

'Will these do?' I proffer the tin to the doctor.

He nods his head and bends down to the amputee. 'Don't worry; these blighters will save your life. What's your name?'

'Bombardier McLachlan, Royal Artillery, sir.'

I swear the man almost lies at attention.

'No, what's your first name?'

He relaxes. 'Gordon, sir. Aye, but most people call me Jock.'

'Why is that?' asks the doctor with a smile. He's good. He may have more patients than any doctor can handle, but he has not lost his humanity.

'It's because… Och! Sir, you'll be taking the—'

'All right, Jock. I'm going to put some of these chaps in your bandage and then dress your wound. Nurse,' he beckons over Solange. 'Change the dressing every eight hours with a fresh batch of maggots.'

Solange nods, but I can see she is cringing at the thought of handling the disgusting creatures. I admire her fortitude; she is a wonderful nurse.

The doctor strips the bandages from the blind soldier's eyes. 'And what is your name?'

'Gunner Jacob Rabinowitz, sir.'

'Well, Jacob, whoever did your dressings has done an excellent job. There isn't much I can do for you here, but back in England you'll get the help you need.'

'Thank you, sir.'

The doctor takes me by the elbow and leads me out of earshot. 'Jewish. Don't let him fall into the hands of the Jerries. They do unspeakable things to Jews.'

'I'll do my best, but they are not evacuating the seriously wounded.'

'They are. But it is all taking time. The houses and chateaux and even the warehouses for miles around have injured soldiers in them.'

The doctor checks Dickie over.

'Do you have anything for the pain?' asks Dickie. 'I'm afraid not.'

The doctor leaves us to tend to thousands more, I'm sure.

Jimmy comes back with two bottles of wine, three loaves of bread, some cheese, and a ham. I am too grateful to ask him where he got them.

I've made a fire from pieces of wood I found. We sit quietly as we eat our meal. The sun has dipped below the horizon and now the chill of the night is beginning to creep in, though the fire helps to keep it at bay.

'Where are you from in Scotland, Jock?' I ask.

'Inverness, sir. We have a small sheep farm up there my wife tends while I am away. I dinnae know how I'll cope with the hills on only one leg if I make it back home.'

Solange rubs her hand along his arm. 'You'll manage. I've seen your courage get you this far. You'll cope with your sheeps on the 'ills.'

I can't help smiling at the way she says, 'sheeps.'

'And Jacob, where are you from?'

'Golders Green, sir.'

'What were you doing before you joined up?'

'I worked in the diamond market. When they declared war, I decided to join up before they called me up. I served my apprenticeship in cutting diamonds, sir.'

'Square pegs and round holes,' I say remembering with gratitude the German artillery spotter and ex-sailor who saved my life.

We bed the three patients down in the horsebox for the night. Jimmy finds a corner and curls up.

Solange leans up against the wall next to me with the remains of a mug of wine in her hand.

'Your shoulder, Harry, 'ow is it?'

With all that has happened, I had forgotten about my injury. 'It's fine, Solange, just fine.'

'It does not look good 'ere, Harry. You should try to get away. I will look after the others until it is decided whether we can go, too.'

'No, Solange. I promised your father I would take you to England, and take you to England I will. The others too. It looks as if there is some semblance of order. In the morning, I'll go down to the mole and see if I can get us all evacuated.'

She puts her head on my shoulder. I put my arm around her.

'I understand now what my Papa told me about the last war. I didn't understand at the time. In war what is important is that you look after your comrades and they look after you. This idea of fighting for your country, 'e said, comes second. I think that is true, 'Arry. They need you in England, but you will not leave your comrades. You are a good man.'

We sit without speaking for a long time. Perhaps both lost in our thoughts of home. And then, as if by telepathy we turn to face each other and our lips touch. It's a soft and gentle kiss. How did this happen? I do not know. It just happened. So little time I have known her and so much I have come to love her. This has never happened to me before, and I have known many women.

'I wish we 'ad met in different circumstances.'

'So do I, Solange.'

We kiss again. We are two lost souls adrift in a catastrophe. Am I deluded by the circumstances or is this real?

Solange stands up, and I, too, stand. By a mutual and unspoken decision, we leave our little enclave and walk hand-in-hand into an empty bombed-out shell of a building. We are alone here and it feels so right. Two lost young people who may not live another day have every reason to give comfort to each other.

An old mattress lies discarded among the ruins. I feel it. It is dry.

CHAPTER FIVE

Friday 31st – May 1940

I wake with my arms around Solange. She's breathing lightly, covered up with my flying jacket. Overhead, I hear the drone of engines. They're German, not British. Solange opens her eyes. I wonder if I will see regret for what we have done. Instead, I see a smile. She kisses me.

'Come on, we need to check the patients,' I say though I want to stay here with Solange and let the world do what it will.

We make our way back to the enclave and find Jimmy already busy boiling water on a fire. Where he got a pan and the makings for a cup of tea is something I dare not ask, nor do I care about right now.

'Mornin', sir, Solange. Tea's up.' He hands us both mugs of hot tea.

It tastes good and warms me from the inside.

Solange takes a few sips and then goes into the horsebox with tea for the injured.

'Sleep well, sir?'

I don't know if Jimmy suspects what Solange and I were doing. Do I care? I suppose I do for the sake of her reputation, but these are strange times. 'Yes, I slept well, Jimmy. And you?'

'Not bad, sir.'

We breakfast on the rest of the bread and cheese. 'Right! I'm off to the mole to see the officer in charge.' The food sits restlessly in my stomach.

I make my way along the beach. Crowds of men sit huddled in small groups around campfires. Others line up in orderly queues either to wade out into the surf or join the long snake that winds towards the mole. Others clamber aboard the small boats coming shore. Suddenly everyone is running or diving to the ground.

Three ME 109s come in from the sea, low, with their cannons blazing. The shells kick up sand. Splashes of blood spread where they hit the prone soldiers. It's a scene from Hell. Screams fill the air above the noise of the enemy's engines. I've faced these planes many times, but I had the facility to fire back at them. There was no time for fear in the fight up in the blue. Down here, I am helpless and scared. Please, God, don't let them hurt Solange.

The Royal Navy ships send up fire, but the 109s still come.

I try to crawl into the sand to bury myself, though sand will not stop a cannon shell. I have no way of fighting back. All I can do is lie here and hope I do not die.

There's a machine gun post inside a wall of sandbags with one man firing a Vickers at the planes and another feeding in the belt. The first 109 kills both men.

Screams still fill the air though the planes have retreated. I see men running towards a line of bodies. The dead lie in neat rows where they fell. The machine gun crew slump over the sandbags. This isn't war. It's murder. We're fish in a barrel. How many men will die before this lunacy is over?

I shake the sand from my tunic as I rise to my feet. My knees shake.

'Where the hell are your lot?' yells a voice behind me. I turn to see a short, scruffy soldier pointing at me. 'Bloody RAF, why aren't they protecting us?'

I know he has a point. Maybe Churchill is keeping them to stop a German invasion. I'm not sure about Churchill. He's only been in charge for two weeks since Chamberlain resigned. But if he is preparing to stop an invasion then he has my vote though a couple of squadrons would be most welcome over this beach.

Shit! The 109s come back, firing away.

Without a plan, I leap into the machine gun post. My critic comes in behind me. I open fire on the first 109 while my short friend feeds in the ammunition belt. It's amazing what the threat of death will do to your senses.

Black smoke erupts from the 109's engine. Above the noise of the plane and gunfire, I hear cheers. I got the bastard! He's heading out to sea but too low to bail out. I haven't time to see what happens to him, as I'm firing at the second 109. I don't hit him. His shells rip through the beach, killing scores more men.

The cannon shells from the third 109 come in a line towards the machine gun post. The sand is red. There's no time for fear. I keep up the rain of bullets at the 109. Yes! I got him. A trail of black smoke follows him, but he keeps firing. My loader and I duck under the sandbags as the cannon shells rip through the post, smashing the Vickers. Well, we got two out of three.

Once the planes are gone, I raise my head above the sandbags and turn to my new friend.

He grins and pats me on the back. 'You're all right for a Brylcreem boy!'

As I look around the carnage on the beach, I struggle to hold back my tears.

I climb out of the post and continue towards the mole. It isn't that I don't care about the wounded and dying; I can do nothing for them. There are plenty of helping hands. It has come down to what Solange's father said; comrades look after comrades.

It's a hive of activity at the mole with lines of soldiers marshalled back into some semblance of order after the panic of the air raid. I can see there is order and discipline now.

I find a naval officer in a pair of sea boots and duffle coat. He's barking out orders to a team of sailors getting the soldiers in line.

'I need your help.'

The naval officer raises an eyebrow. 'And we need the bloody RAF. Where are they?'

'Attacking the Germans inland, like I was before I was shot down.'

'What do you want?'

'Passage to England, what do you think?'

'So you're a pilot.'

'Yes.'

'Go to the front of the queue on the second ship along there.' He points to a rusty twin-funnelled steamer moored to the mole.

'I have a wounded pilot and two wounded Royal Artillerymen, plus an able-bodied RASC and a nurse. I need to evacuate them.'

'No chance! You're priority, not that it seems fair, so get yourself aboard. The others will have to take their turn. We'll get them off if we can, but we are taking the able-bodied first. Churchill is going to make a stand in England, and we need all the men we can get, including your lot.'

'I'm not going. I won't leave without them.'

'Look, you RAF chaps may think you are high and mighty, but there's a war on, and you have to do what is best for the country. Now get yourself aboard that ship.'

I turn to walk away. Suddenly, two burly sailors grab me from behind and drag me along the mole. They elbow several soldiers on the gangplank out of the way and shove me aboard the steamer. I try to trip one of them but they hold on to me too tight.

One of my captors calls to a big sailor with a black beard and a belly that suggests he has not seen his feet for a while. The fellow comes over. My captor explains that I will stay below and secure.

I can hear grumbling about the RAF among the soldiers on the ship. We do not seem popular. That's so bloody unfair after what we have done and what Larry sacrificed.

'Sorry, sir, but orders is orders,' says the big sailor as he propels me across the deck in an arm lock.

I'm not having this. I won't leave the others in the lurch. With a supreme effort, I break free, dash to the seaward side of the ship and look down. It's a long way, but it must be deep enough to take the ship.

The bearded one is right behind me. I leap over the gunwale and land feet first in the water. The shock of the cold hits me like a punch from a heavyweight champion. I go under and struggle back to the surface. It isn't easy swimming in a uniform tunic and flying boots. I cast a glance up at the ship. Lines of soldiers peer over the side, cheering. I don't know why. They've spent ages trying to get on board, and this idiot has jumped off. Maybe they're glad the RAF is staying behind.

With great effort, I manage to swim to the shore and make my way back to our enclave.

'Mon Dieu! What 'appened?'

'I thought I'd take a swim to cool off. We won't be going via the mole. Jimmy, they will take you. Go down to the mole and get yourself in line to board one of the ships.'

'With all due respect, sir, no! I'm not running out on you and the others. And that is my final word on the matter, with respect, sir.'

'But you have to get back to your wife and child.'

'Indeed I do, sir. But I'm still not going so you can put me on a bloody charge if you must.'

I nearly well up in gratitude at this salt of the earth man. All I can think of doing is offering my hand for him to shake. He takes it. Even more evidence that Solange's father knew about comrades.

'Right then, we have to think of a way to get us all off here. Any ideas?'

'I saw some pleasure boats and a few fishing boats taking soldiers off the beach out to the big ships. I heard rumours that Churchill has sent out every small boat from England they can muster. We could try one of those, sir.'

'We could get the injured onto one of the smaller boats I think, but we'd never manage to transfer them aboard the bigger ships when we get out there. We may have to rely on getting them off via the mole though that is not possible for the time being.'

'I'll go see what I can find out, sir.' Jimmy heads off down the beach.

'You'd better get out of those wet clothes, Harry.'

With little privacy, I strip off and wrap my nether regions in a blanket and my top in my flying jacket. It's fortunate I was not wearing it when I jumped overboard, or I would have gone down like a stone. Solange hangs my uniform up to dry.

I hear engines again. Coming in low from the west, I see a Junkers JU 88 flying parallel with the beach. He's not firing. Still he comes almost low enough to touch. Now he's climbing. Suddenly a massive explosion rips through the air. Just in time, I manage to duck behind the wall and pull Solange down with me.

A thick cloud of sand rushes heavenwards from his bomb. I hope Jimmy is safe.

The soldiers on the beach all clamour to help the dying. They can do little for the dead. This is a nightmare, but I'm not asleep. God help us.

Jimmy returns unscathed. 'A beach master is organising the evacuation by the smaller boats. He told me they are only taking the able-bodied and walking wounded out to the big ships because loading the badly injured is too slow and difficult.

The wounded have to go via the mole when they are ready to take them. Some of the larger small boats are taking soldiers all the way back to England. That's the best way we could evacuate the three patients. But the beach master would have to be persuaded.'

'Well done, Jimmy. I'll go and see him.'

'He's about two hundred yards down the beach. Be careful, sir. I don't think a blanket and a flying jacket is going to impress him.'

Jimmy is right. I sit on the ground in front of the fire and wait. The sun lacks warmth. I'm impatient for my clothes to dry.

Solange busies herself with the patients.

Another night creeps in. Jimmy's powers of purloining supplies have dwindled, or perhaps the availability has diminished. That's hardly surprising, judging by the number of men stranded on this beach, even after the air raids and casualties. As fast as men leave the beach, it fills up again. The lines of people on the mole continue to snake towards moored ships like a ghastly host lit by moonlight. Other lines, at significant risk of drowning, trudge through the sea to waiting ships too big to come in close. All along the beach are fires. There's no point in enforcing a blackout. It reminds me of Dante's Inferno.

Solange makes our patients comfortable and then we go back to our love nest in the bombed-out building. How strange it is to find love in the midst of this carnage. We may be dead tomorrow but tonight we have each other.

CHAPTER SIX

Saturday 1st June 1940

Another day dawns on this desperate scene. I can't understand why Hitler has not sent in the Panzers and Luftwaffe to finish us off completely. We've had air raids and shelling but nothing on the scale that I would expect after they succeeded in herding us all into a small killing zone. All it would take are two or three squadrons of fighters, a couple of bombers and a few Panzers and that would be the end of the British Expeditionary Force. What is Hitler up to? There must be a reason for his holding back.

Solange opens her eyes and smiles. It's strange but I'm glad I'm here at Dunkirk with her. Maybe in normal life, she would be way out of my reach, but here in this hellhole, we are all equals. I find myself being drawn closer and closer to her. It might be soppy, but I do believe I have fallen in love. It may be she feels the same way about me too though neither of us has said it aloud.

The best we can manage for breakfast is some stale bread. Jimmy has obtained bandages and antiseptics for Solange to treat the three wounded. He may have stolen them, but I am not going to inquire. It's enough that he's risked so much to get them for us.

It's a dull day. In the distance, I hear artillery. It's closer than yesterday.

I set off down the beach to find the officer in charge of loading the small boats. I find him, a naval lieutenant commander, surrounded by army officers demanding priority. He does not look the type to bully as he stands there in his sea boots, stroking his black beard while puffing on a pipe. His team of sailors chivvies up the lines to board the small boats. Some of them look seriously overloaded.

A Junkers JU 88 comes in low. Everyone except the beach master dives or runs for cover. He stands and looks up at the intruder, shakes his head and returns to a sheet of paper he has in his free hand. A mad Englishman. That's why I have hope we can overcome this immediate threat to the United Kingdom. Eccentric fellas like this one who refuse to dive for cover will stick two fingers up at Hitler. I'm not eccentric, but I take this opportunity to jump the queue as the enemy plane closes in.

The Junkers doesn't open fire or drop a bomb. Perhaps he's just on reconnaissance to report to Goering. No. Further down the beach he opens fire on a line of men wading out into the sea. Why? Cold-blooded murder.

I take advantage of the confusion to press my case. 'I have three stretcher cases, one able-bodied soldier, a nurse, and myself to evacuate. Can you help me?'

He shakes his head. 'RAF. You ought to keep your head down, lad. You chaps are none too popular along here. I know your people are hitting the Hun south of this debacle but these chaps don't. They think you have abandoned them. I'd like to help but you'll have problems getting the stretchers aboard the ships out there from these small boats.'

'Could we get on one of the boats that are going all the way back to Dover?'

'Well, you're a pilot, yes?'

'Yes.'

'The orders are to make you a priority so I can load you but not the rest of your group. To be honest, the way it's going, I doubt they will get off before the Germans come.'

'But I need to take them all off. I can't leave any of them.'

'Sorry, but no can do. You'd best get yourself back to Blighty damned quick because they're going to need you.'

'Thanks anyway.' I walk back along the beach with my heart in my shoes, or so it feels. Am I failing my duty to my country by not abandoning my people?

Maybe I am. But a little voice in my head tells me I'm doing the right thing. I can't go back to the mole, or they may succeed this time in keeping me onboard.

We spend the rest of the day sitting around. Though it started dull, the day has brightened up. Dickie, Jock, and Jacob seem to be doing well. Jacob doesn't say much. I think he's scared that he's blind. I don't blame him for that.

Further up the beach, I can hear a Scots piper playing a lament. Jock has tears in his eyes. Solange has worked wonders with his leg. His chances of survival, if I can get him back to England, look good.

As the evening comes and the sun sinks, quietness hangs over the beach like a shroud. Are we all doomed? I will get all my people home. I will. I will.

Perhaps those still out there on the beach believe their chances of getting off are slim. That's why they are so quiet. Quiet as lambs awaiting slaughter. In the last rays of light, I watch a line of men wade out to a black and white paddle steamer similar to the one sunk by the Stuka. I've seen this type of boat on the Clyde and the Isle of Wight taking holiday-makers on day trips. How long will it be before any of us have a holiday? A long time, I think.

Dickie, Jacob, and Jock are back in the horsebox. Solange, Jimmy, and I share the last of a bottle of wine he acquired as we sit cross-legged next to the fire.

Four scruffy soldiers stomp into our little enclave.

'You got booze, mate?' says one of the soldiers in a northern accent.

'None left,' I say.

'Pity,' he says. 'You got a woman though. You gonna share her?'

'What? Get out of here!' I jump to my feet, and as I do, I draw the Webley. Too slow. The soldier lands a punch on my jaw knocking me backward to crash into the wall. I feel dazed.

'Grab her,' says a voice.

I try to move forward, but my head feels as if it is spinning. A soldier grabs Solange and then he yelps.

Solange has stuck a pair of scissors in his neck. He's bleeding heavily.

I gather my senses and smash my fist into the one who spoke. Then I kick him in the groin.

Jimmy grabs his Lee-Enfield and points it at the men. 'Fuck off, or you'll be staying under the sand.'

'I'm bleeding,' moans the scissored man, holding onto his neck. I think Solange missed the artery by fractions of an inch, though if he doesn't get medical attention he may bleed to death.

I shake my head back to sensibility and pick up my Webley. 'Get out of here.'

The men go. Discipline is breaking down. It's getting more and more dangerous to stay here. We must get off.

Jimmy and I take turns at keeping watch while Solange sleeps between us in our little enclave. There will be no love nest tonight.

CHAPTER SEVEN

Saturday 2nd June 1940

This is the fourth day we've spent here. Without washing facilities, we are all beginning to ripen. Solange works wonders keeping the patients clean with the little water we have. There isn't enough for all of us to wash and washing in the sea just makes the skin sticky with salt.

There's more artillery fire coming onto the beach now. And we've had more air-raids. I think Jerry must have finally decided to wipe us out.

The beach and surrounding streets lie littered with debris. The mole still takes its never-ending line to the ships. Men wade out into the sea. Small boats skim the shore line and pick up soldiers to take out to the big ships or carry their passengers all the way to England. It is an absolute disaster but one that will go down in history as a miracle because so many men will make it home.

I must ensure that my small party is among them.

A dull routine has settled over Dunkirk, broken occasionally by the mind-numbing terror of air-raids and shelling. We must get off soon. Surely the Germans must be close. The rumour is that the French have taken over the defensive ring to allow the British to escape. If that is true, then God bless them. And God help them.

I decide to move our party down to the shoreline in the hope of getting aboard one of the small boats going back to England. It's risky. The RAF is not popular due to the lack of air support. Solange is one of the very few women I have seen in the past few days and by far the most attractive. I just hope the sergeants can keep discipline. To be fair, most of the soldiers are showing signs of resignation and are keeping good order. Just a few hotheads getting out of control. They would be the troublemakers down the pub on a Saturday night, back home. Every army has them.

Dickie sits up in his bed in the horsebox. I lean down to him. 'Dickie, I'm thinking of moving the three of you down to the shoreline to see if we can get aboard a small boat. Are you up to it?'

'Of course, Harry. I feel so bloody useless lying here. I wish I could do something to help.'

'You can, Dickie. I'm going to take you first. Solange will stay with you. If I give you a pistol, do you think you could use it, if it came to it?'

'What, in case some idiot has designs on Solange? Yes, of course, Harry. My legs are broken, not my arms.'

'Thanks, Dickie.'

He's done well. No complaints from him though he must be in agony with his internal injuries. Had the doctor taken him from the chateau he would have stood a better chance of evacuation rather than rely on my feeble efforts. I haven't seen the Major, Doctor Driscoll, or the rest of his party. Perhaps they have already managed to get off. Or maybe they are in one of the outlying houses or chateaux to await the Germans. Perhaps Dickie is better off with me after all. Who knows? It's academic if I can't get us away.

Jimmy and I carry Dickie down to the shoreline to a point a hundred yards this side of the beach master. Solange stays with him. He fingers the pistol, and I know he'll use it if he has to. It's good to see Dickie back in charge. He could lose both legs and still beat you to death with his fists. We are going to need people like him in charge if we stand any chance of winning this war. I hope he pulls through. He will pull through. Dickie doesn't know the meaning of failure, and he instilled that in me too from the first day I met him. Over the last few days though, with him out of action, I'm not sure that determination to succeed on my part was always prominent.

Jimmy and I return for Jacob and carry him down. He's afraid because he can't see anything, but he stays stoic as he has done throughout.

Then we bring Jock.

With all three stretchers laid out on the shoreline, all we need now is for a boat to come in close so we can commandeer it. There are groups of men milling around with the same idea. If the beach master sees what we are up to, he'll have me arrested.

Fortunately, the clouds have come over, and there's a light breeze coming in from the sea, so we don't need shade for the patients.

I see a small cabin cruiser coming in. I reckon it's around a thirty-footer with a long cockpit. If that comes in close, we could get our people on board. There's jostling, and murmurs behind me as groups of soldiers seem to have the same idea.

Jimmy still has his rifle. I retake my pistol from Dickie. I hope this does not turn into a shooting match. It's not just that we would lose; it would be a terrible stain on our military if the soldiers became a mob. I can see further up the beach where the soldiers are in neat lines just waiting their turn. I don't know why these chaps behind me have decided to queue jump. Well, perhaps I do. We are trying to jump the queue. We haven't slipped into it being every man for himself yet, but I think that moment will arise soon.

The cruiser comes in. The bow runs aground. I have to smile at the skipper. He wears a blazer and grey flannels with a peaked cap that has an anchor badge. He would be more at home coming down the Thames to the Henley Regatta rather than crossing a sea in wartime.

Before I can do anything, a band of around ten soldiers dash past me into the water and board the small boat. We have no chance to get aboard. The skipper puts the engine in reverse and drags the bow off the beach.

Boats are coming in and out all the time, mainly up by the beach master, but a few come inshore near us, though we have no chance of jostling anyone out of the way.

A fishing boat comes in. It is mainly open with a small cuddy at the bow. It must be a good forty feet long. This is a working boat, not a pleasure boat like the last one. The skipper of this one looks professional. He wears a fisherman's smock, smokes a pipe, and has a big grey beard. This one would do fine for us.

The skipper beckons to us to come out to him. Suddenly there is a dash from behind and six soldiers are in the water around the boat. We've lost that one, too.

They drag the boat closer. I see my short machine gun loader is one of them. Cocky little bastard!.

I have my Webley and Jimmy still has his rifle but I don't want to shoot anyone. Not in these circumstances. I can understand the desperation of these men but I haven't sunk that low, yet.

Shorty wades back to me. 'Want a hand, mate?'

I can't believe it. We're going home!

The squaddies carry Dickie out to the boat and then come back for Jock. God bless them!

Jimmy and I climb aboard to help settle Dickie and Jock. Solange kneels on the beach next to Jacob. She's stroking his arm. It must be terrifying if you can't see what is going on around you, only hear the sounds. I hope they can do something for him back in Blighty.

A creeping barrage of shells comes down the beach but stops about a hundred yards from us and then creeps back the way it came. Safe for the moment.

Jimmy and I jump over the side and wade back to the beach. A 109 comes from the seaward side with all guns blazing. I see the trail head for Solange and Jacob. I'm too far away to do anything.

'Look out, Solange!'

She can't hear me over the shelling.

The trail of bullets from the 109 rips through Jacob knocking him sideways. Solange has blood all over her. Is she hit?

Jimmy and I make it to her side. She's frozen to the spot in shock but the blood isn't hers. It's Jacob's. He's dead as mutton.

'Solange, Solange, you are all right. Come with me, quickly. Jacob is dead. We have to leave him.'

I pull her to her feet. She's dazed. I don't think she knows what is happening. Our boat waits for us. Everyone on board is yelling and waving at us to hurry up.

'Get back aboard, quick, Jimmy. I'll bring Solange.'

The barrage creeps down the beach towards us again. Stukas dive-bomb the mole sending the soldiers scattering. Some dive into the water. A bomb hits a ship. It blows up in a ball of flame.

Out at sea, I see a Stuka dive-bomb the small cruiser with the Henley Regatta skipper. I want to call out a warning, but nothing can be heard over the din of battle. The bomb hits the water behind the boat and sends up a plume of water. The boat rocks but doesn't capsize. Missed, you bastard!

Two more Stukas attack a destroyer. She's sending up flak. Yes! Got one of them. The Stuka's scream is less scary now it has a trail of smoke behind it. The pilot can't pull out of the dive. It hits the sea and explodes. Thank God it missed our boats.

The creeping barrage comes back along the beach and stops fifty yards short this time. Shrapnel whistles through the air. Better get Jacob and Solange aboard quick. I turn away from the bloody scenes around me and focus on my companions.

Everywhere around me men are ducking for cover, splashing into the sea, and battling for their lives. Forget the Jerries! Death has us in its grasp now, and it's all we can do to escape.

The beach fills with flying shrapnel from the barrage. I hear it zing through the air. Just one of those pieces would cut someone in half.

Solange falls to the ground. No! I scramble to her side; I'll have to carry her. I grab her right hand and throw her over my shoulder in a fireman's lift. The soldiers on the boat wave and shout. I know, we must hurry! Two of them point to the sky.

I look up. Overhead is a Junkers.

I watch a bomb fall as if in slow motion.

CHAPTER EIGHT

Netley Military Hospital near Southampton, England
Tuesday 4th June 1940

Where am I? I look around. This is a hospital bed. I'm in my own room with a glass door looking out onto a corridor. I smell disinfectant. Have I lost any limbs? I move my toes and my fingers. They seem to be there. I can see. What happened to her?

My mind drifts back. All I remember is being on the beach, carrying Solange over my shoulder and everything going black.

Where's Solange? What happened to Solange? I try to sit up. My head hurts. In my arm is a tube. Am I in a German, French, or British hospital? I can see through the windows on the other side of the corridor to the outside. I know where I am. This is Netley Military Hospital near Southampton. I made it home!

I see Jimmy outside in the corridor. He's on crutches.

He hobbles in. 'You're awake at last, sir. You've been out cold for a couple of days.'

'Where's Solange?'

'She didn't make it, Harry. I'm so sorry.' He puts his hand on my shoulder and then sits on the bed. 'A bomb went off and I got a lump of shrapnel in the leg. You were knocked out. The lads dragged us both aboard but Solange, well, I'm afraid she was done for.' Jimmy continues to talk but it's as if I'm listening to a foreign radio station. 'Two of the lads went back for her but they were killed in the barrage. She didn't stand a chance, Harry. They had to get the boat away before it was hit by a shell or bomb. It was bloody murder out there. I'm so sorry, Harry, er, sir.'

'Solange, dead? I can't believe it. Are you sure?' My world has just fallen in. I force myself to think back again, to remember what happened. I can't.

'Harry, I saw her lying on the beach after the bomb and then when a shell went off and killed the poor sods who went back for her, well, I'm so sorry.'

I don't know what to say. I feel so numb that I can't even find a tear. This can't be true! She can't be dead. Solange was so full of life.

A Queen Alexandra's Nurse comes in. 'Flying Officer Fitzpatrick. You're awake. That's good. The doctor will be along soon to give you some tests.' Her uniform reminds me of Solange and it manages to draw a tear that I don't bother to hide.

'Dickie made it. He's in a London hospital,' says Jimmy.

I'm happy that he got home but the emptiness inside me is nowhere near filled with this piece of good news.

Jimmy sits with me while I wait for the doctor. He tells me he has had a visit from his wife. We sit in silence after that. There's nothing to say.

After a thorough going over by a kindly old gentleman of a doctor, I'm put in a wheelchair and wheeled off to the main hall by an orderly. Jimmy hobbles along with me.

In the hall, I see scores of injured soldiers. What's going on?

A doctor in a white coat fiddles with the dials on a wireless on the stage. 'Quiet everyone. This is Winston Churchill's speech to Parliament today.'

The BBC newsreader reads out Churchill's speech.

'We shall go on to the end, we shall fight in France,
we shall fight on the seas and oceans,
we shall fight with growing confidence and growing
strength in the air,
we shall defend our Island, whatever the cost may be,
we shall fight on the beaches,
we shall fight on the landing grounds,
we shall fight in the fields and in the streets,
we shall fight in the hills;
we shall never surrender, and even if, which I do
not for a moment believe, this Island or a large part

of it were subjugated and starving, then our Empire beyond the seas, armed and guarded by the British Fleet, would carry on the struggle, until, in God's good time, the New World, with all its power and might, steps forth to the rescue and the liberation of the old.'

A great speech but I don't care. I just want to go home. Nothing matters now that Solange is gone.

* * *

I'm glad to get out of the hospital. They've been very good to me over the past three weeks but I don't think I could stay there any longer. It is so depressing with all the injuries our lads have suffered. They said I had a severe concussion and have to rest before going back to my unit so they've sent me down here to Hastings to recuperate. I just want to get back in the air. They say time heals wounds. I'm sure it does for the physical ones but I don't think the loss of Solange is a wound that will go away, ever.

I get off the train at Hastings and find a car waiting for me. The driver is a dapper little fellow with a pencil moustache. He must be in his fifties. He's RASC, like Jimmy.

The transport is a green painted Austin. The image of the Hispano-Suiza flashes through my mind and Solange sitting beside me.

I hope Jimmy enjoys his home leave. Maybe I'll see him when I can go up to London to see Dickie. I'll never see Solange again. I can't wait to get back in the air and avenge her.

'Flying Officer Fitzpatrick?' says the RASC soldier.

'Yes.'

'Come with me please, sir.'

We drive along the coast road and come to a sizeable country mansion. This is not bad for a convalescent home. The grounds are well-kept and full of trees and flowers. The building is substantial. I'm not really interested. Nothing seems to lift me since I heard about Solange. The driver leaves me at the impressive entrance between two stone pillars.

A nurse stands in the doorway. 'Welcome. You are Flying Officer Fitzpatrick?'

'Yes.'

'Please come with me.'

We go through a marbled hall to a carved wooden staircase. I see an Aphrodite statue on a plinth at the foot of the stairs. It's not an original. I can tell that. It reminds me of the Pandora statue at Solange's chateau. There are so many things that keep coming back to remind me of her.

My room is on the first floor. It's comfortable and I have a view of the sea. The nurse leaves me to settle in. I watch the activity down on the beach. They're laying mines and barbed wire. The invasion is expected. This may not be the best place to be when it comes. The last time England was successfully invaded was near here in 1066. Let's hope the coming one fails.

I have to get better so I can do my bit. They said at the hospital my concussion needs to be settled. Apparently my brain is bruised. I just wish it was wiped of all the painful feelings I have. Stop feeling sorry for yourself. You have a job to do.

* * *

The drawing-room of this house seems a little out of kilter with the rest of the building's Victorian and Edwardian furniture. In here someone has used flair and imagination to set it up in Art Deco. All style and no comfort. I sit in a leather armchair with a back that's too low and read the Daily Telegraph. France has surrendered. The Germans are in Paris.

'Flying Officer Fitzpatrick, your trunk call to Belfast is ready, sir.'

'Thank you,' I say to the white coated orderly and follow him.

He takes me into a small office at the side of the entrance hall. There's a desk with a black telephone off the hook. The orderly leaves me alone and closes the door.

I pick up the phone. 'Hello?'

'Harry!'

'Hello Ma.'

'How are you? We were so worried.'

'I'm fine Ma, just fine. How are you and Da?'

'We're all right, Harry. Are you injured?'

'No Ma, just a bit shaken up. I'll be convalescing for a few days.'

''Can you get home to see us?'

'I don't think so, Ma.'

'They said we didn't have long to talk so here's your Da. Take care, son.'

'Hello, Harry. How's it going?'

'All right, Da.'

'You sure you are all right?'

'Yes, Da.'

'Harry, I know what it's like.'

'I know you do, Da.'

The sound of home and what happened in France comes down on me like an avalanche. I can't hold it in any longer. I can't talk for the sobs and slump into the only chair.

'I know, son. Let it out. Don't try the stiff upper lip. That doesn't work. Believe me.' The timbre in his voice tells me he's crying too.

* * *

After a wash and brush up in my room I'm almost under control. I take dinner in the dining room with stern looking figures looking down from their portraits at the ten officers using their table. Dinner is quite palatable after Netley's mass catering but I still have little appetite. Deep inside I have this sense of failure. I failed Solange and her father. I will never forgive myself.

We have three naval officers, four army officers and three RAF pilots. I think I recognise one of the army officers, a captain. He has lost his left arm but I'm sure it is him. He doesn't seem to recognise me but I'm not surprised at that. He was very busy the last time I saw him.

After dinner, we split up. Some go to the library and others outside to smoke and take in the evening air. I follow the captain, who seems to have decided to take a walk around the grounds.

'Excuse me, captain.'

'Yes.'

'Were you at Dunkirk?'

'Yes. That's where I lost the wing. Last damned boat out and we took a hit. But most of me got back so I have to be grateful for that.'

At least the chap has retained his sense of humour.

'Dreadful business.'

'Yes, were you there?'

My thoughts drift back to the last time I saw Solange. 'Yes, I was there.'

'Thank God and Churchill. Between them they got most of us away.'

'You are a doctor, I believe.'

'Yes.'

'You treated one of my party. A young Jock who lost part of his leg and had gangrene.'

The captain says nothing for a moment and then he nods. 'Yes, I remember. Maggots! Did he make it back?'

'Yes, he did.'

'Good. He was lucky to have the French nurse. She knew what she was doing. She saved more than a few lives that last day too. I hated leaving her behind. She wouldn't come. Insisted on staying behind to help the wounded.'

'The last day? You mean the fourth? Solange was killed on the second.'

'Sorry my mistake. Or, no, did you say Solange?'

Suddenly my stomach churns as if I were on the rollercoaster on Blackpool Pleasure Beach as I realise what may be. 'The nurse, on the fourth, the last day of evacuation, do you know her name? Was it Solange?'

'Solange, yes. Are you all right? You'd better sit down.'

'Please, this is important. I have to get it straight. Are you saying that Solange was alive on the fourth?'

'Well, a nurse I knew as Solange, was, yes. I could have sworn she was the same one with the maggots. You don't forget a woman who looks like her. She wandered into my makeshift hospital totally disorientated from the bombing and shell fire. She's a very brave woman. She pulled herself together and helped me with the injured. She said she was going home if the Germans would let her. I hope they do. She had an inner sadness, poor woman. I think she had lost someone very close to her though she never said anything about him.'

I grab his one hand and pump it up and down. 'Thank you, thank you.'

'I say, steady on, old boy!'

Through the gardens I race to the beach. I have to stop at the barbed wire.

Overhead, silhouetted against the moonlit clouds, I see three Spitfires heading out to sea. Maybe they are on their way to France. The rumble of the Merlin engines is unmistakable. The Hurricanes are good but the Spits are great. I shall retrain and join one of their squadrons.

France will be free again. I look out into the Channel. About fifty miles over there is France—and my Solange.

'I'm coming back for you, Solange!'

Sign up to know when
the second book
in the series is launched

www.DashforDunkirk.com/secondbook/

DENIS CARON

Denis Caron was born in Trenton, Ontario, grew up in England and returned to his native Canada, where he now lives in Kitchener, Ontario.

His working life has been varied. After earning a college diploma in survey engineering, he went on to serve in both the Canadian army and Air Force, travelling to a wide variety of distant places such as Bosnia, Greenland, Senegal, and the Middle East. He now works for the emergency services.

Denis' great interest in the military and in WWII, was the catalyst that attracted him to write a book. His novel, a fictional story set during the period of the Second World War, is his first and he enjoyed the experience enough to want to take up writing as a full-time career.

When he has time to spare, Denis loves to indulge in his hobbies of sampling craft beers, travelling around Europe and adding to his growing collection of WWII memorabilia. He also likes to relax with a good movie.

He appreciates any feedback or comments and can be reached at Denis@DashforDunkirk.com

FRAN CONNOR

Fran Connor is British and lives in beautiful SW France with his wonderful wife Viv, their dog Molly and chickens. He claims he's living in that area for the lifestyle and weather which he says helps an author's creative juices. It may just be an excuse to drink wine and lounge in the sun. He writes novels, nine published so far with more coming out soon.

You can visit him at www.connorscripts.com